Vd

B

D1118248

BLOOD ON THE SAND

Mav, on his way west from Tennessee, encounters a gang of desperadoes about to kill a young Apache brave. When he intervenes to save the victim he stirs up a lot of bad blood — but he also forges an unusual partnership when a band of Comanche comes to his aid. He rides on the small town of Cimmaron hoping, at last, to find some rest . . . but he soon discovers that there are more surprises left in store for him yet . . .

LEE LEJEUNE

BLOOD ON THE SAND

Complete and Unabridged

LINFORD
Leicester

First published in Great Britain in 2010 by
Robert Hale Limited
London

First Linford Edition
published 2012
by arrangement with
Robert Hale Limited
London

British Library CIP Data

Lejeune, Lee.
  Blood on the sand. - -
  (Linford western library)
  1. Comanche Indians- -Fiction.
  2. Western stories. 3. Large type books.
  I. Title II. Series
  823.9′2–dc23

  ISBN 978–1–4448–0951–0

Published by
F. A. Thorpe (Publishing)
Anstey, Leicestershire

Set by Words & Graphics Ltd.
Anstey, Leicestershire
Printed and bound in Great Britain by
T. J. International Ltd., Padstow, Cornwall

This book is printed on acid-free paper

1

He was on the Eimarrow cut-off south of the main Santa Fe Trail. He was headed in the general direction of California, Los Angeles, maybe: The Place of the Angels. The man some called Mav didn't believe in angels but it was a good picture. Didn't believe in El Dorado or rivers of gold either, but maybe they held out a ray of promise, even to a saddle bum like Mav!

He was riding a good strong horse called Huckleberry and trailing a mule that had no particular name but that didn't matter since the mule knew what to do when he asked it and did an excellent job without being called anything but 'Mule' or 'Mule Without a Name'.

Mav. A strange figure riding a roan on a dusty trail towards who-knows-what? He had a cactus-like growth of beard and a hat that might once have passed as a fedora though now it was somewhat bashed in and grey with grime and dust. Might have looked right on the turnip head of a scarecrow back east in Tennessee!

Yet, under the stained brim of the once-had-been fedora, there were two intense blue eyes narrowed with concentration. Not the eyes of a scarecrow. Not the eyes of a man easily scared. Not the eyes of a loser either!

He knew the trail. An old timer had told him about the various landmarks he might find interesting and useful. These included the unexpected springs and water holes along the way. He was headed for one right now. He could see the stand of trees that marked the spot.

Huckleberry's nostrils flared and his ears pricked. The mule who was called Mule gave a sudden discordant ee-aw noise.

'You got it, Huck,' Mav said. 'You got it good. That refreshing smell is the smell of water. We nearly got there. We can wade in and take our fill. Grass too. This thing you can smell is horse heaven, mule heaven too.'

At the edge of the stand of trees he dismounted and led Huckleberry in between the willows. Mule needed no pulling. They say a mule is stubborn and headstrong but this four-legged beast needed no bidding.

Mav undid Huck's cinch and removed his saddle. Then he took the weight of his worldly goods off the mule's back. Within less than a minute the two animals were at the water side slurping at the reviving elixir of life.

Mav began to strip off his clothes, first his fustian jacket, then his vest, and his boots. He unbuckled his gunbelt and laid it aside clear of the water and within easy reach in case of emergencies. The old timer had warned him about Comanche and Apache and Kiowa. Maverick figured there was little danger but a man had to take care. 'Always expect the unexpected,' the old timer had said before he sent a long stream of tobacco juice into the spittoon.

Mav dipped his toes in the edge of the pool and found it good. Mighty good! He started wading in deeper and would have lain on his back and luxuriated. This was the answer to a saddle bum's prayer. He chuckled, then stopped and listened. Huck raised his head from the water and stood with his nose dripping and his ears pinned back.

'What's that? You hear something?' Mav said to the horse.

No question. The ground shook with the thunder of hoofs and the sound was getting closer.

'This needs investigating,' Mav said. He scooped up his gunbelt and strapped it on. He pulled on his boots. He drew his Winchester from its sheath. He picked up his battered hat and stuck it on his head but let the rest of his clothes lie where they were on the ground. 'Stay there, boys, and keep you quiet,' he advised.

He made his way to the edge of the

trees and peered out between their branches. He saw a single rider followed by a bunch of other riders. One, two, three, four, five, he counted. Five against one, that's bad odds. He screwed up his eyes and peered out from under his battered hat. This was five men in pursuit of a single Indian, an Apache as far as he could make out. He had left his telescope in his saddle-bag but it didn't matter: the Indian was getting closer all the time, riding hell for leather towards the stand of trees where Mav was crouched as though waiting. As the Indian got closer Mav saw he was nothing more than a raw youth, sixteen or seventeen, maybe. The bunch riding after him were no Indians. They were white gringos, or Mexicans maybe, and they were sure intent on riding down that boy and doing him harm.

As Mav worked his jaw and watched, two things happened. Puffs of bluish smoke sprang out from the pursuers and were snatched away into the air. A moment later, he heard the pop, pop, pop of gunfire. Those gringos, whoever or whatever they were, were aiming to bring down the young Indian and possibly kill or maim him. 'The only good Injun is a dead Injun,' as General Sheridan said and these guys were following that piece of army wisdom!

The second thing that happened was that the Indian's pinto caught its hoof in a gopher hole and came crashing down. The young Indian brave hurtled over its head in a somersault and landed on his knees in the dust. But this was some Indian. He was up on his feet in a moment and turning to face his pursuers. He had a Bowie knife in one hand and a tomahawk in the other.

His pursuers reined in and came to a ragged stop. Then they paused to consider matters . . . from a cautious distance.

Mav saw that four of the men had their shooters out, but the fifth, slightly ahead of the others, had taken a huge stock whip from his saddle horn and was dangling the tip in the dust with serious intent on the boy.

'Seems you took your long last run, eh, Injun boy?' he said.

The boy snarled and squared up with his tomahawk raised.

'Looks like it wants to make some kind of stand,' another of the pursuers said with a laugh. He was a big, beefy *hombre* who looked like he'd been stuffing corn and red meat into his gullet for several generations.

The other three riders sidled up to watch the fun. One kept his shooter out. The other two holstered their guns and rested back to watch how things might develop.

The one with the stock whip gave a high peal of laughter, something between a cackle and a coyote call. Unlike the others he was well spruced up and dandified as though he shaved every morning and took a bath in rose petals whenever he could. That was why they called him Coyote Ben, though Mav didn't know that till later.

7

'Watch this, boys,' Coyote Ben said. 'Take account of a man of skill and learn something.' He raised the whip. It snaked out like a flash of lightning and circled the Indian boy's wrist. Coyote Ben gave a dextrous twitch of the whip, the tomahawk spun out of the boy's hand and pitched into the sand. 'How's that?' Coyote Ben boasted.

His sidekicks hooted with laughter and thumped on their saddles to show their appreciation.

'That's real good, Coyote,' the beefy *hombre* said. 'Now comes the next trick. Watch this.' He drew his shooter, a Colt with a long barrel, cocked it, and took aim on the boy.

But this was one brave Indian boy! Before Big Bravo could fire, the Bowie knife sped through the air and took the sombrero from his head. A quarter of a second later Big Bravo fired but the shot went high in the air on account of Big Bravo dodging to avoid the blade.

All the bunch were rocking with laughter in their saddles, except Big

Bravo who was cocking his gun for a second shot, which could turn the Indian into dead meat.

The Indian boy glanced at the stand of trees where Mav stood watching and decided to make a run for it. But Coyote Ben was one quick dude. The stock whip streaked out again, took the boy by the ankle and jerked him off his feet.

'Now see him dance,' Coyote Ben said as the rest of the bunch hooted with laughter again. 'Dance, little Injun, dance!' he said, lashing the Apache boy across the back with his whip.

Mav saw the Indian wince and quiver with pain, but he didn't cry out as he dragged himself to his feet.

That is some Indian boy, he thought to himself.

'You want to dance, tyee? You want to dance, boy wonder?' Coyote Ben roared as the stock whip lashed the sand all round the Indian.

The Indian danced involuntarily to avoid the pain of the lash.

Big Bravo got the message, caught the fever, and started gunning down on the kid with his long barrelled Colt. Dust spouted up all round the kid as he danced to avoid being hit. The other three riders also caught the fever. One of them fired straight at the boy and pumped a bullet clean through his arm.

The kid gripped his shoulder and sprawled face down on the dust, wounded and gasping with pain and exhaustion.

There was a momentary pause. The riders edged close and looked down at the Indian.

'Want me to finish him off now?' a thin scarecrow character called Broken-wheel asked, cocking his weapon.

'Hold on! That's my privilege,' Big Bravo said.

He calmly dismounted and strode over to the boy, turned him with the toe of his boot, cocked his shooter and stuck it against the kid's head.

The kid shook his head and Mav saw that he was all in.

He stepped out from behind the willows and raised his Winchester. 'Stop just where you are!' he said. 'You pull that trigger, that will be murder, mister.'

The whole bunch seemed to freeze, as if the deep frosts of winter had suddenly come upon them. Big Bravo still had the pistol against the boy's head.

'You want to take that shooting-iron away from the kid's head and drop it good and easy on the dust,' Mav sang out. He had a Southern drawl, as though he was from somewhere in Mississippi or Alabama or some place East.

He saw the heads of all five of the bunch turn to look at him, and he knew he looked kind of strange, like the wild man of the plains, in his battered hat and his long johns, wearing cow-puncher boots and a gunbelt.

Coyote Ben was shaking with derisory laughter. 'You just got out of bed, Calico?' he jeered.

'Drop the gun, mister.' Mav motioned with the Winchester to Big Bravo. 'Let it down real gently on the ground.'

Big Bravo exchanged quick glances with Coyote Ben. First the Indian with the tomahawk and now this weird figure from the willows. Was he to look a fool for the second time?

'Can you handle that danged thing?' he roared.

Mav had his head tucked down. He was looking along the barrel, getting Big Bravo into his sights. 'You want to try me, mister?'

Big Bravo glanced at Coyote Ben a second time and Mav read the message.

'Don't come too close with that stock whip of yours,' he drawled. 'Not if you want to keep it in the family.'

Coyote Ben watched him steadily, like a snake getting coiled up ready to strike. 'You think you can take all of us at once, big talker?' he said.

Mav nodded but kept his eye on Coyote Ben. 'One at a time will do,' he said.

Brokenwheel gave a nervous titter. That's the one that's trigger happy, Mav thought. Big Bravo was now drawing himself up to his full six foot four. He held the long-barrelled six-shooter pointing slightly forward at the dust.

'Like I said, drop that shooter on the ground,' Mav said.

'You want to commit suicide?' Big Bravo said.

'I'll take a chance on that,' Mav said. 'If someone has to go, you'll be the first one.' He motioned with the Winchester again. 'I'm gonna ask you one more time, mister. Drop that gun and ask your cowboy friend to lower that stock whip of his and tuck it away before anyone else gets hurt.'

A quietness descended on the trail, but it wasn't the quietness of peace. A hot wind crept over the plain with a faintly menacing whine. A curl of tumbleweed came bouncing along behind the bunch of men trying to make up their minds whether to shoot or back off.

You can see by a man's eyes when he intends to gun down on you. The most important eyes in the bunch were those of Coyote Ben, Mav figured. He saw them shift quickly at Big Bravo and then return. Something in their depths seemed to relax slightly — a dangerous moment.

Coyote Ben shrugged. 'OK, Injun lover, what do you propose?'

'I propose you leave this Apache boy and ride off nice and easy. That way nobody else gets hurt,' Mav said.

'If that's the way you want it.' Coyote Ben gave a twisted grin. 'OK, boys, you hear what the man says. Seems he wants to keep the Injun for himself. Not worth a cent piece anyways. Ain't that so, Big Bravo?'

Big Bravo did not deign to reply but he moved real slowly to holster his weapon. 'You watch your back, mister,' he said. 'This business ain't finished yet.'

'That's right,' Brokenwheel echoed. The other two said nothing but they

14

looked like skunks with their own stink in their nostrils.

Big Bravo mounted up. He wheeled and turned to face Mav. 'You heard that, mister,' he said. 'From now on you watch your back. The thing that goes bump in the night could come at any moment to take you off.'

The five of them gave a rumble of ragged laughter. Then they all rode away.

* * *

Mav watched them ride away until he was satisfied they wouldn't wheel round and come back on him. Then he turned his attention to the young Apache lying gritting his teeth in the sand. He knew from past experience that no Indian likes to show weakness and pain and would even prefer to die with his teeth clenched than to cry out. This Indian brave was no exception. As Mav bent over him his eyes came round to him like a cornered beast.

'Steady there. Hold on,' Mav soothed.

He knelt beside the boy and examined the wound. It had struck the shoulder high but there was no exit wound which meant the bullet was lodged there, not too far from the bone.

'We need to get you back there in the shade,' Mav murmured as much to himself as to the Indian. He tried to summon up what little Apache he knew. 'You Tinde.' He tapped the boy on his good shoulder. 'Me, help you, get you right.'

The light of understanding came into the boy's eyes. He clearly knew a little English.

Mav helped him up into a sitting position. The Indian gestured towards his mustang lying a little further off, fatally wounded. Mav understood.

'OK, you want me to look after your pony?'

He left the boy to sit where he was. He walked over to the pony. It was a good pony but it had no chance of survival out here. Its eye flickered to

Maverick and he shot it right through the head. He picked up the boy's tomahawk, then retrieved his Bowie knife.

He laid them like an offering beside the boy.

'Now we go,' he said. He put his arm round the boy's shoulders and helped him on to his feet. The boy stiffened but managed to struggle towards the willows. He stood looking at Huck and the mule without a name. Then he lowered himself beside the pool and stretched out. Mav had scooped up the tomahawk and the Bowie knife and he laid them down close to the Indian again.

He wasn't much of a talking *hombre* but he talked a deal to his horse on the trail. Stopped him from going plumb loco, he reckoned.

Having stared at the stranger for a moment, the horse had resumed his eating where the grass was lush at the edge of the pool.

'What am I set to do?' Mav said to

the horse. He stood for a moment in deep thought beside the pool. 'Guess you're right there,' he said. 'I got to light a fire before sundown and get that bullet out of the boy's arm before it turns bad. No use rescuing an Indian like that and letting him die on you.'

The Indian boy was staring at him and shivering slightly.

'You OK, kid?' Maverick said. He didn't expect an answer but the kid's lips moved and he spoke.

'Good,' he said.

'Plenty good,' Mav agreed. 'Got to get that shoulder right.'

The kid nodded. It seemed he understood.

'You speak English?' Mav asked him.

'Little English,' the Indian said.

'That's good,' Mav said. 'Makes things a deal easier here.'

He gave the kid a drink from his canteen and sparked up the fire.

'You're gonna get pain, plenty pain, when I dig that bullet out of your shoulder but I'm gonna give you a good shot of whiskey to dull it down a bit. You savvy?'

What a waste of good whiskey, he thought, but that's the way it's got to be. The Apache boy took the whiskey, pulled a wry face, but gulped it down.

'Don't get the taste for it too much,' Mav warned him, but the kid accepted another slug. Maverick found a suitable length of willow branch that the kid could clench his teeth on. Mav wasn't too well-versed in surgery but he dug deep. The Indian boy clenched his teeth on the willow branch and almost bit right through it, and, though he quivered with pain, he kept himself from lashing out.

The bullet came out clean and there was a deal of blood. Mav poured more whiskey on the wound to cauterize it and then bound it up as best he could from a spare shirt he had in his baggage.

'That's a job well done, Huck,' he said to the horse. 'Now we gotta take our rest and sleep.' Strange how inflicting pain on others can make you weary, he thought.

He opened a can of sardines and a can of beans to mark the occasion. The Indian seemed to be off his chow a little. So Mav finished off what he couldn't eat.

After that the kid slept. Mav threw a horse-blanket over the boy and turned into his bedroll, keeping his shooter close by.

Mav had never rhapsodized over the great outdoors but those stars twinkling through the trees gave him the feeling he had done a good job rescuing the Apache boy from those ornery *bandidos* and patching up his wounded shoulder. So he slept in trust and peace.

★　★　★

When he woke quite suddenly, the boy was standing over him with his tomahawk poised in his hand.

You damned fool! Mav thought, trusting an Indian with a weapon close by. But the Apache boy raised his good hand with the tomahawk and motioned him to keep quiet. Could be those *bandidos* had come back again, Mav thought. But, when he reached for his Colt, he knew it was something else.

The silent form of another Indian was framed in the trees. Not one but one, two, three, and more.

The Indians stood looking down at Mav and the Indian boy. They were not menacing or wild-looking. They were standing still as figures carved out of the rocks, and Mav knew they were not Apache. They were Comanche!

2

Mav got up on to his feet real slowly. He kept the Colt trailing in his hand in case the Comanches got the wrong idea. The Comanche warriors had their arrows pointing directly at him and some carried Winchesters. So he figured raising that Colt could be a very bad deal. He raised his left hand and said: 'Peace.'

The leading Comanche took a step towards him and spoke in good English. 'Been watching you,' he said. 'Saw what you did to those other moonfaces.' He turned to regard the Apache boy. 'Saw you save this Apache papoose.' His lips twisted in a grin of derision. Mav noticed that his skin was slightly paler than the skin of most Comanches he'd seen. Comanches were usually short, squat men with bow legs from spending most of their years on horseback. This man was taller and slimmer, though well-muscled.

'Rising Cloud,' the man said. 'Chief Rising Cloud.'

'You can call me Mav,' Mav said. 'I greet you with much pleasure, Chief.'

Rising Cloud nodded abruptly and his lips curved slightly.

'You speak good English,' Mav said.

The chief nodded again. 'I learned it good. My mother was Scot. But she talks Comanche mostly now.'

Mav turned his head to look at the Apache boy who was still holding the tomahawk in his good hand. He looked as though he was ready to swing it in a second and slice down the chief. But the chief was wary and his braves had their weapons trained on the boy.

'Not much to offer, Chief,' Mav said. 'But why don't I stir up the fire and we can sit around and parley a little?'

Chief Rising Cloud looked thoughtful. 'What do you plan to do with this Apache?'

Mav shrugged his shoulders. 'Like you saw, he got wounded in the shoulder. I did my best for him. That Apache is brave. If he's a papoose, he's a papoose with much courage.'

Chief Rising Cloud gave a grunting laugh. 'The Tinde, the Apache, are our enemy,' he said. 'We fought many battles with them and we defeated them. They ride like little children. We ride like men. We take many prisoners.'

Mav nodded. 'This boy deserves to ride free, Chief. He's young but he shows much courage. I know the Comanche respect courage in a man.'

At that moment, as if to contradict the point, the Apache boy winced and gripped his wounded arm. For half a second Mav feared the chief might mistake his move and slice him down with the knife he had on his belt.

Then another thing happened; a warrior stepped out from behind a tree and Mav saw it was a woman. She walked forward and stood beside the chief. They held a brief conversation in

Comanche. Mav wasn't too familiar with Comanche customs but he knew that, among them, women were respected. A woman could become a chief and own many horses.

Rising Cloud nodded and turned to Mav. 'This is Water-that-Runs-in-the-Creek,' he said. 'She is a great healer. She wants to look at the boy's wound.'

The woman spoke quietly again to the chief.

'Water-that-Runs-in-the-Creek says she can see from the boy's looks he has a bad infection. She wants to give him healing,' the chief said.

Mav turned to the boy and saw that he was in no state to resist. 'Tell Water-that-Runs-in-Creek that we thank her and tell to go ahead.' He looked at the boy and saw he might agree. 'This Water-that-Runs-in-the-Creek will look at your wound, give it healing,' he said.

The boy sat down and bared his arm.

Water-that-Runs-in-the-Creek knelt down beside him and spoke reassuring words. She obviously had a little Apache.

While the process of healing was taking place, Chief Rising Cloud and Mav sat down by the water. Mav stirred the fire into life. Some of the other Comanches stood close but didn't squat down with the chief and Mav. Others were hovering about keeping a close eye on the surrounding scrub.

'You got good whiskey?' the chief asked.

'Not much,' Mav said. 'Used most of it on the boy.' He had heard that any strong liquor could have a bad effect on Indians. Something in the blood, he guessed. He reached in to his saddle-bag and produced the bottle which now contained no more than an inch or two of whiskey. He handed it over to the chief. 'Keep it,' he said.

The chief held the bottle up against the light and shook it. 'Bad medicine,' he said and stowed the bottle away in his medicine bag. 'How many good horse you got?' he asked.

'Just one,' Mav said. 'That's Huck over there. And a mule too but mules 'don't count for much.'

'We have many horses,' the chief boasted. 'Good strong horses. They ride many days on the prairie without stopping.' He shook his head. 'Many good horses. You ride far?' he enquired.

'California maybe,' Mav said. 'I aim to pick up the Old Spanish Trail and carry on right through.'

The chief nodded again. 'California is a long long way, so they tell.'

'Maybe too far,' Mav conceded. 'Maybe not.'

They might have said more but there was a movement among the trees and one of the braves keeping watch ran up, jabbering quickly in Comanche. The chief rose and barked out an order. The whole bunch of Comanche braves were snatching up their lances and mounting their horses. 'Tinde!' they murmured, pointing out across the scrubby plain.

Mav threw his saddle over Huck's back and secured the cinch. He rode out to the edge of the stand of trees and drew in a little to the right of the chief.

The Comanche were lined up on their impressive palominos facing south from where another line of riders were coming close. The Comanche were a small force, no more than ten, eleven including the woman who was still tending the boy beside the water.

As the Apaches approached, Mav saw there were more. He counted up to twenty and there could be others coming in from another direction. The whole cavalcade lined up facing the Comanches as though for battle. Mav could see from their long flowing hair and their smocks tied in at the waist that they were Apache.

For a long tense moment the two lines of warriors stood facing one another with their weapons ready. Those Comanches were more than handy with the long deadly lances they carry but they generally speared down their enemy when they were on the run. The Apaches carried short bows and muskets and a few Winchesters. So it could be a bloody encounter.

'What do you aim to do, Chief?' he asked Rising Cloud.

The chief stared unwaveringly ahead for a moment. He didn't want to be distracted or caught off guard.

'Maybe we fight,' he said.

'What about the boy? They might think we want the boy.'

Rising Cloud nodded slightly. 'The boy is our prisoner,' he confirmed.

Mav considered matters. 'You speak Apache?' he asked the chief.

The chief gave him a quick sideways glance. 'I speak a little Apache,' he said tensely.

Mav nodded. 'This could be a good chance to improve your language skills,' he said. 'I'm gonna ride out and do parley with those Apache.'

He eased his heels into Huck's sides and rode forward a pace or two. The Apache chief, wearing black and ochre smears of paint across his cheeks came forward a little to meet him.

Mav held up his hand in greeting. 'Peace,' he said.

The Apache raised his arm and rode forward cautiously. 'Peace,' he said. 'You Comanche?' He was grinning disparagingly. Anyone could see from Mav's battered hat and his cactus face that he was no Comanche.

'I stand between the Comanche and the Apache,' he said.

The Apache chief gave a brief nod. 'Running Antelope is your prisoner.'

How am I going to explain this? Mav wondered.

Now Rising Cloud was beside him, speaking partly in Apache and partly in Comanche and partly in the sign language the Indians of different tribes used to communicate. Mav could see he was telling the story of what had happened to the Apache boy pretty well.

The Apache chief listened in dignified silence for a while. Then he nodded abruptly and spoke in Apache.

Rising Cloud turned to Mav. 'He says he wants to see his son Running Antelope here in front of his eyes.'

Rising Cloud turned in the saddle and barked out an order. The woman healer Water-that-Runs-in-the-Creek emerged from behind the trees accompanied by the boy Running Antelope with his arm in a sling.

The boy looked pale and drawn but at least he could stand on his feet and walk. The Apache chief released a babble of questions. The boy answered sullenly as though he felt he had acted like a coward in riding away from his pursuers and getting himself shot.

Mav had heard enough. 'That is one very brave boy,' he piped up. He started filling in the details about what had happened earlier. He pointed out the carcass of the dead horse and tried to explain how the boy had attempted to defend himself from Coyote Ben and Big Bravo and the rest with his tomahawk and knife. Mav had never thought of himself as particularly passionate or skilful with words but he pieced out the whole story with gestures and pointing and the Apache chief seemed to understand, especially when the boy Running Antelope supported the story in his own language.

One of the other Apache warriors brought up a spare horse and they helped the kid to mount up.

The two ranks of warriors stood with their feathers fluttering for a moment longer. Then the Apache chief raised his hand and said: 'Peace.'

Rising Cloud raised his hand and said: 'Peace.'

The Apache warriors turned in perfect order and rode away. The Comanche were reputed to be the best riders on the plain, but these Apaches were pretty good too.

Mav groaned with relief.

★ ★ ★

Well on along the trail, Coyote Ben and Big Bravo were close to the town of Cimarron. Coyote Ben was in the lead with Big Bravo on his heels. The other three, Brokenwheel, Jim Sivers, and

Rawhide were several paces behind. Big Bravo was still fuming somewhat from the events of the day before.

'We should have killed that ornery Apache Injun,' he mumbled. 'Like the General said, 'the only good Injun is a dead injun'.'

Coyote Ben nodded his agreement. 'We could have killed him sure,' he said. 'But that would have meant shooting that Injun-lover who looked like a scarecrow escaped from a funny farm. That could have been difficult. He might have looked like he was waiting for a flock of blackbirds, but my guess is he could have brought two of us down before we finished him. Anyway' — he flung back his head and spoke over his shoulder — 'we keep looking, let Fate decide; that pleasure might come later.' He fingered the stock whip draped across the horn of his saddle.

'That pleasure is coming to me,' Brokenwheel hooted. 'I got a feeling about it.'

Big Bravo was not impressed. 'Your

feelings! What are those, little big man!'

Jim Sivers and Rawhide tittered with laughter until Brokenwheel snarled at them, 'Shut your big mouths, blabberchops!' They knew if Brokenwheel had a mind to shoot a *hombre* he would draw a gun and kill him without a qualm. Something to do with the thin man's upbringing, Jim Sivers figured.

Coyote Ben was grinning to himself. 'OK, boys,' he said. 'Like you promised Bravo, if we meet that scarecrow something's gonna go bump in the night, that's unless I get there first with my friend here.' He stroked the stock whip and patted it. Coyote Ben had a big love affair going with that stock whip.

'I have a real good idea, Coyote,' Rawhide said. He was a short, dumpy guy with straggle of beard on his chin.

'You have a good idea!' Jim Sivers marvelled. 'That must be worth a couple of bucks at least.'

Rawhide gave a derisory laugh. 'OK, big mouth, you keep sounding off like that one day someone's gonna stuff one of those jokes down your big gullet right down to your arse!'

'They like to try, I'll shoot his guts so full of holes he'll be like a pepper pot.' Jim Sivers retorted.

'What's your big idea?' Bravo enquired.

Rawhide looked like a man who could solve the world's problems with one throw of the dice. 'I figure we could rest up some place and wait until that scarecrow comes riding by. That way we could all take a shot at him and leave him for the wild coyotes and the buzzards to rip apart and eat.'

'That's a real dumb idea,' Jim Sivers jeered. 'That scarecrow might never pass by on this trail. You want to hang in there till the crack of doom?'

The other four shook with laughter.

Coyote Ben said. 'That's good, Rawhide, but I figure we should ride on in to Cimarron. Take things easy. They got a bank, so I hear. We don't want to waste bullets gunning down on a scarecrow when we could be getting richer in a bank, now do we?'

'You got a point there,' Bravo said.

★   ★   ★

Rising Cloud had taken something of a liking for Mav and they rode along together with the other Comanches strung out behind. Water-that-Runs-in-the-Creek was close behind the chief. Mav glanced at her once or twice and saw she was a real handsome woman, somewhere between thirty or thirty-five summers. It was difficult to tell. It was clear that Rising Cloud and the braves respected her as a woman of means, with many horses, but she spoke no English and restricted herself to a few low phrases in Comanche.

The chief glanced sideways at Mav. 'You set to make camp with us?' he said. 'We make a big feast.'

It was a tempting offer. 'I aim to hole up for a piece,' Mav said. 'Like you said, it's a long way to California. Maybe I should aim for Santa Fe, or somewhere closer. They tell me there's a little town called Cimarron not too far off.'

The chief raised his eyebrows. 'We have a big feast,' he said.

Mav had a thing about offending people, especially Indians and particularly Comanche. So he accepted the chief's offer. They debouched from the trail and rode through the day until, before sunset, they came to an encampment under the lee of a small hill. There were no more than ten tepees of various sizes.

The chief dismounted and conferred with Water-that-Runs-in the-Creek.

'You rest here,' he said to Mav. 'We take care of your horse and the mule. Feed them real good. That horse is a very good horse.' He patted Huck's flank and ran his hand over the horse's shoulder.

Mav stooped into the tepee and dumped his baggage on the ground. This unfamiliar environment interested him but, as soon as he stretched out on the rawhide sleeping place, he sank into a deep sleep.

* * *

He woke to the sound of drumming and rattles. Outside in the open space between the tepees they had lit a fire and the warriors sat around it, chanting and drumming. Mav reached into his bag for a mirror and scraped away at his beard with a Bowie knife. It wasn't as good as a razor but it would be good enough until he reached Cimarron. It seemed more respectful to the Comanche to shave his cactus jaw.

Several of the young braves chuckled when they saw his clean, lean jowls but Rising Cloud held up his hand to stop them.

Mav was not a well-practised dancer but he joined in the merriment through the night. Even Rising Cloud deigned to grin and give an encouraging wave. As the dancing continued, Mav perched beside Rising Cloud. Water-that-Runs-in-the-Creek brought a pipe and they smoked sweet grass together.

Water-that-Runs-in-the-Creek knelt and laid a pair of fine beaded moccasins at Mav's feet. 'For you,' she said in English.

Those handsome moccasins were a rare gift.

Mav went into the tepee and fumbled in his baggage. He produced a silver pendant, the only thing of value he had. He had meant to give it to a girl back East but she had run off with a big trader in cotton goods and silks, so that had come to zilch!

He laid the pendant in the hands of Water-that-Runs-in-the-Creek and her eyes lit up with delight. Rising Cloud also looked pleased. He would probably have liked to have the pendant for himself.

'We are brothers,' he said to Mav solemnly. 'You go to Cimarron and we keep you in our hearts.'

3

The town of Cimarron sat close to the Cimarron River. It was small, near the Raton Pass and consisted of a bank, a thriving general store, the Cimarron Grand Hotel, a Butterfield stage depot, and a sprawl of cabins. When Coyote Ben, Big Bravo and the others looked down on the place they had mixed feelings.

'That place ain't worth a dime,' Brokenwheel complained.

'Don't fret yourself,' Coyote Ben said. 'There's a bank there, as I said. Where there's a bank I smell money, greenbacks and silver. Never despise a small town with a bank.'

'We can take it. No trouble at all,' Big Bravo agreed confidently.

'Heard tell the sheriff's real mean,' Rawhide said. 'Name of Bill Harding. Shoots from the hip, no questions asked.'

'That's no never mind to me,' Big Bravo said. 'The bigger the sheriff, the harder he hits the sidewalk.' He patted the long-barrelled Colt on his hip. It was like the Buntline special Wyatt Earp had used in the shoot-out with the Clanton bunch. This was no quick-draw stuff. You just kept your nerve and levelled the weapon, and *bam*! Big Bravo had already shot down a dozen men, some of them fatally, and even Brokenwheel treated him with caution. You could never tell what a big man with a gun could do if he felt so inclined, especially when he had an uncertain temper like Big Bravo.

They rode into Cimarron, eyeing the place up and down and from sidewalk to sidewalk, five dusty, hard-bitten *hombres* who looked as if they had drifted in through the murky gates of hell.

'What do we aim to do, kick around here for a while?' Rawhide asked.

'Nothing,' Coyote Ben responded. 'We just rest up, feed the horses good, take a bath, maybe, and ease our weary bones a bit.'

'What about after that?' Rawhide insisted in a tone of impatience. It was clear he was thirsting for some kind of action.

'Then we make a decision,' Coyote Ben said. 'Maybe we ride on to Santa Fe like we planned. Maybe we just take the bank and ride off into the sunset to count the loot.'

That gave rise to another ripple of laughter. 'I heard somewheres they got a good line in dancing girls at the Cimarron Grand Hotel,' Jim Sivers put in.

'Where d'you get your information?' Brokenwheel asked.

'I read the papers when I get the chance,' Jim Sivers said. 'Find them blowing about with the tumbleweed. One mentioned beef dinners and dancing girls at the Cimarron Grand Hotel. Thought it sounded appetizing.'

'Yeah, and I hear they got a particularly nice floozie set up specially for you,' Big Bravo said. 'And a big six-foot-seven girl for me. They call her Brassy Baby.'

'Brassy Baby sounds about your measure,' Coyote Ben said.

'Brass right through,' Big Bravo agreed. 'Just the way I like 'em.'

They reined in outside the Cimarron Grand Hotel which looked a deal more shabby than grand. An old timer rocking himself on a rocking-chair in the porch got up real quick for a geek and disappeared into the hotel as fast as his creaky legs would carry him.

'Looks like they're expecting us.' Coyote Ben laughed.

They tied their horses to the hitching rail and ambled inside. A man in a red-and-gold fancy vest was sitting behind the reception desk totting up figures in a register. When he looked up he saw Big Bravo staring down at him like a cross-eyed mountain bear.

'What can I do for you, gentlemen?' the reception clerk enquired nervously.

Coyote Ben elbowed his way forward.

He was much shorter than Big Bravo but he had a kind of authority and he knew how to speak. 'We want the best room in the house,' he said. 'A big room with five beds will do.'

'Well, let me just see what we have available,' the clerk replied. He started fumbling through his booking list. 'I fear we're almost fully booked up at the moment. There's a party coming in on the Butterfield stage this very afternoon; two or three ladies, I understand. I believe they booked the best room; that's the one on the top floor. Yes . . . yes.' He ran his finger down his reception list.

There was a dull thud on the counter. The clerk looked up and saw Big Bravo's Buntline Special resting there with Big Bravo's hand on it. 'Put those floozies in another room!' Big Bravo said. 'We got here first, didn't we?'

'I don't think I can rightly do that, gentlemen,' the clerk stammered.

Big Bravo reached across the counter,

took the clerk by his vest with two hands and lifted him clean out of his seat. 'Can't you arrange that for me, little man!' he snarled.

The clerk turned as pale as cream cheese. 'Yes, sir. Yes, sir, I'll see what can be done, sir.' He fumbled with his booking register and his hands were trembling so much he could hardly turn the page 'Oh, yes,' he said. 'I think we can make a switch. I'm sure those ladies will accommodate you.'

'Just like Brassy Baby!' Jim Sivers sniggered.

The five men laughed, none too pleasantly.

'If you'll be kind enough to sign the register,' the clerk said.

'Gotta see the room first,' Big Bravo demanded. 'You don't pay for the goods up front till you see them.'

The clerk turned even paler, as though he might be about to pass out. Then he gulped in a breath and recovered himself a little. 'If you'll be kind enough to come this way,' he said.

As he ducked out from behind his desk, trying to make himself as small as possible and led the way up the dusty stairs, a woman in a flamboyant gown with purple-dyed hair stood waiting. She was wearing shoes with tottery high heels and looked almost as tall as Big Bravo. Big Bravo swept off his dusty hat and bowed low with mock courtesy. 'Good day, madame, and who would you be?' he asked.

'I'm the Queen of Sheba, and who would you be?' She grinned like a painted doll.

'I'm the fastest gun in the West,' Big Bravo rejoined. 'Pleasure to make your acquaintance, ma'am.'

The painted doll gave a sniff and passed on down the stairs, and Jim Sivers and Rawhide emitted whistles and hoots of ribald laughter.

'This is your room, sir,' the clerk said. 'All aired out just this morning. Clean sheets and everything.'

He slid to one side as Coyote Ben

strode past him and inspected the room which was long and narrow and contained three beds.

'Thought I said five beds,' Big Bravo boomed. 'I count but three.'

'Oh, don't worry about that, sir. I can have another two moved in right away. We aim to please our clients every way we can.'

'We'll take our chow downstairs at around eight,' Big Bravo said. 'Table for five.'

'Yes, sir.' The clerk was backing out through the door. 'I'll see to it, sir.'

'What a dump!' Brokenwheel pronounced.

Big Bravo was already sitting on what he took to be the best bed, pulling off his boots and emptying a pile of dust on the floor. Jim Sivers was bouncing on the bed he had chosen, raising another cloud of dust.

'Just like home!' Rawhide complained.

'Guess I might bide on the floor here,' Brokenwheel said. 'Not used to sleeping in a bed . . . specially with bed bugs!'

★   ★   ★

In the early evening the five men trooped down the stairs and ranged themselves along the bar. They had spruced themselves up somewhat but they were still wearing their shooting-irons. In a room adjacent to the bar someone was already tinkling on a piano that badly needed tuning. At the other end of the bar a big man in a black floppy hat was hanging over a bottle of whiskey. When he turned to glance in the direction of the five men, Coyote Ben saw the glint of a star pinned to his vest. This must be Bill Harding, Sheriff of Cimarron. The clerk in the red-and-gold vest was leaning close to him, talking earnestly into his ear. When Coyote Ben glanced in his direction, the booking clerk shrank away and disappeared through a side door.

The sheriff continued with his bottle of whiskey for a while but Coyote Ben knew he was there propping up the bar with one purpose. The management had called him in in case of trouble. He was packing a pistol not too far short of Big Bravo's. Coyote Ben was good at smelling out dollars, but he also had a nose for trouble and could see big trouble at the end of the bar.

Presently Bill Harding turned casually towards the bunch and tipped his hat on to the back of his head. That was another bad sign. He was thickset to the point of stoutness. He wore long trailing moustaches, of which, by the look of things, he was extremely proud, and he had an annoying glint of confidence in his eye.

'You boys come from far?' he asked casually.

'Quite a piece,' Coyote Ben said. 'Been riding some days right through Comanche Injun territory.'

'That so,' the sheriff said with a hint of mockery. 'See many Indians?'

'We saw Apache,' Brokenwheel piped up. 'A whole bunch of them came riding down on us but we drove them off.'

'Superior gun power,' Harding mocked, glancing down at Big Bravo's Buntline Special.

'We killed a few,' Jim Sivers boasted.

That made the sheriff grin. 'You want to know something, gentlemen,' he said. 'This town of Cimarron is small. We don't have much to offer, but we do have one thing. We're a peaceable community here and we don't care too much for trouble.'

'Hope you tell the Injuns that next time they come in to trade,' Rawhide suggested.

The sheriff nodded slowly as though he saw some hidden reference in the comment. 'You boys aim to stay long?' he asked.

'Long enough,' Coyote Ben said. 'That's if you don't have any objections.'

'That's no big deal,' the sheriff said, 'just as long as you mean to keep the peace.' He slid his empty bottle along the bar towards the barman, crammed his hat firmly on to his head and made for the door.

Rawhide and Jim Sivers began to cackle and punch one another around.

A waiter all in black appeared at the door with a white napkin draped over his arm. 'Your food is ready gentleman, if you'd be so good.'

The said gentlemen would be so good. They followed the waiter to a long table set out specially to accommodate them.

'This ain't so bad,' Rawhide said.

'Serve up the chow!' Big Bravo bawled. 'Bring on the whiskey!'

The piano player, Raunchy Bob, struck up a hearty tune.

'Louder, louder!' Big Bravo shouted. 'I like it loud!' After dinner he would dance. He knew the steps. He intended to dance with Brassy Baby, the Queen of Sheba, all night if necessary, just to humiliate her.

★ ★ ★

When the cocks started to crow next morning four of the beds in the long room were occupied. Every one of the bunch was asleep, except for Big Bravo who was still taking it out on Brassy Baby, who didn't appear to have much objection, and Coyote Ben, who crawled out of bed and sent his floozie off to another room.

While the other members of the bunch went on snoring and Big Bravo was busy taking it out on the Queen of Sheba, Coyote Ben put on his clothes and riding-boots and sent his stock whip out in a long loop where it cracked like the noise of doomsday. Everyone sat up in bed.

'What the hell!' Brokenwheel yelled from the floor where he he had spent the night.

The other painted ladies quitted the room real fast, holding sheets over them to hide their modesty. Big Bravo and Brassy Baby stayed on; they were in no hurry to part company.

'What you do that for, you big ape?'

Big Bravo demanded from his striped pillow.

'Got to make an early start,' Coyote Ben said. 'Got a lot of riding to do.'

The boys dragged on their clothes, pulled on their boots and stood ready. When Coyote Ben cracked his whip they knew he meant business. *A lot of riding* could mean a lot of things, not all of them actually in the saddle.

So they filed down the rickety stairs and took their breakfast, ham and beans and eggs over easy. When they were almost through, Big Bravo emerged, looking none too pleased.

'I don't go for that,' he said to Coyote Ben. 'When I'm in the middle of important business I don't like to be disturbed.'

'Sit yourself down and have some chow,' Coyote Ben said. 'They do a nice ham here and the eggs are fresh.'

Big Bravo was about to draw up a chair when Brassy Baby appeared at the bottom of the stairs. 'What are you doing here?' she demanded.

'I'm about to start breakfast,' Big Bravo said. 'That's what I'm doing.'

'Don't I get no consideration?' the girl asked. She was dressed up in her fancy clothes and she had already applied her war paint. She made the mistake of coming right up to the table and glowering down at Big Bravo. The night might have been long but it hadn't been a bed of roses.

'Sure you get consideration,' Big Bravo said. He got up from the table and gave her the back of his oversized hand across the mouth. 'That's your consideration. That's a present and a thank you from Big Bravo!'

Brassy Baby was tough, but she wasn't that tough. She fell back, doubled up and with her hands over her face. Blood came spurting through her fingers and she moaned.

Coyote Ben and the rest of the bunch looked on in amazement. Big Bravo sat down calmly and attacked his ham and beans and the eggs done over easy.

'The deal is this,' Coyote Ben said. 'Big Bravo goes into the bank with Rawhide and Jim Sivers. While they're doing the business, I stand just inside the entrance and keep lookout, and Brokenwheel takes care of the horses.'

'That sounds OK,' Big Bravo said thoughtfully. He was still glowering like a devil from hell. The incident with Brassy Baby had annoyed him, not because of what he had done to Brassy Baby but because the rest of the bunch had watched in amazement without saying a word. 'As long as we get equal cuts.'

'Sure you'll get your cut,' Coyote Ben promised. 'We all stand together in this outfit. That's what we agreed and that's the way it's gonna be.'

Though they were talking in low voices, the old geek who had been rocking on the rocking-chair on the porch of Cimarron Grand Hotel when they rode in happened to be standing close by and he heard most of what was said. Though his legs were creaky, he ran like a man twenty years younger to the sheriff's office.

'Mr Harding!' he gasped.

The sheriff was a man who liked to be up good and early to greet the day, His wife had cooked him a wholesome breakfast of kidneys and beans and he felt full and comfortable and ready to meet the day.

'What's the problem?' he asked.

The old-timer was pointing with a shaking finger down the street. 'It's them!' he shouted. 'Those men who rode in yesterday. I just heard them talking. They mean to rob the bank.'

Harding knew the old man well and thought he was a gossip-monger. But he reached out for his gunbelt and strapped it on. 'Is this some kind of a joke?' he asked.

'No joke, mister. This is the real truth. I just heard them talking about it. You better come quickly. I reckon they're doing it right now!'

The sheriff took his hat and crammed it on his head. He never went anywhere without that hat. He took a Winchester down from the rack and checked it and stepped out on to the sidewalk.

*   *   *

Big Bravo was at the counter with Rawhide on one flank and Jim Sivers on the other. Big Bravo had his long barrelled Colt out, pointing at the teller. 'Just fill that gunny sack with dollars and silver and everything else you've got and do it nice and easy, just in case my trigger finger gets nervous,' he said.

'Is this some kind of a joke?' the teller asked.

'Yeah,' Big Bravo roared. 'We do real good jokes around here!' *Bam*! The bullet went clean through a pane of glass and into the door leading to the manager's office. The manager was taking down a file behind his desk when the forty-five bullet lodged itself in the oak filing cabinet, sending showers of wood and glass every which way. The manager ducked down behind his desk, thinking there was an earthquake or something.

The teller was so busy stuffing greenbacks and silver coins into the gunny sack that his fingers couldn't move fast enough and he almost collapsed behind the counter.

★ ★ ★

As Bill Harding hurried along the sidewalk clutching his Winchester with the old geek shouting nervously into his ear, he heard the muffled thud of the shot and saw Coyote Ben standing beside the door of the bank with his stock whip in his hand. You don't rob a bank with a stock whip, Harding figured, raising the Winchester to get a bead on Coyote Ben.

'Get away from the door of that bank!' he yelled.

'Who says so?' Coyote Ben laughed.

Bill Harding was about to say: I say so! when two things happened almost simultaneously. The stock whip snaked out just like it had a life of its own and Big Bravo came out through the door of the bank with his Buntline Special raised.

The stock whip curled round Bill Harding's Winchester and dragged it from his grasp.

'What the hell!' Bill Harding shouted. He reached for his pistol and *bam*! *bam*! Big Bravo fired two shots from the top of the steps.

Bill Harding didn't have a chance to cock his weapon. The second shot raised him clean into the air. He fell with a thump on his back with his fingers still twitching on the butt of his gun. Blood poured from his mouth as he tried to raise himself.

Big Bravo moved to the top of the steps, took two strides down and gave the sheriff another shot through the side of his head. Bill Harding's head jerked back and lolled sideways. His blood dripped from his gaping mouth into the dust.

'That one's for the scarecrow!' Big Bravo roared.

Coyote Ben almost said, 'No need for you to shoot that man, I could have tripped him off his feet with my whip,' but he just coiled up the stock whip, mounted his horse, and the whole bunch of them rode away.

4

When Mav rode in to Cimarron on Huckleberry trailing the mule without a name a couple of days later he found a town in mourning. He rode right up to the Cimarron Grand Hotel and dismounted. He was dusty and in need of lowering himself into a hot bathtub but he looked a deal neater and less ridiculous than he had when he met Big Bravo and the bunch on the trail. The old geek, name of Skinny Billy, was rocking on his rocking chair on the porch as usual but this time he didn't get up and disappear inside. He just gawped wide-eyed at the stranger as he dismounted and secured his horse and his mule to the hitching rail.

'Ridden far?' Skinny Billy asked in a high pitched tone as Mav considered whether to walk into the Cimarron Grand.

'Just about as far as from Saint Louis to New Mexico,' Mav replied with a grin. 'Is this the only place in town to bide?'

'Only place worth a nickel,' the old man squeaked. 'Apart from the Widow Bean's. She takes in travellers from time to time, so I hear. But she's just about at the end of her run. Hasn't got a bean she's named for.' The old man chuckled and sent a stream of tobacco juice across the sidewalk into the dust of the main drag.

Mav gave a brief nod. He had his hand on the door and was about to press on when the old timer spoke again. 'You chose a bad time to arrive, mister,' he said.

'That so?' Mav said. 'How can that be?'

'Can be because they killed the sheriff day before yesterday,' Skinny Billy told him. 'Shot him down dead outside the bank. Bill Harding was famous for his quick draw but he didn't get the chance before he was shot down on this occasion. They got him lying in state down there in the funeral parlour. Burying him tomorrow with full ceremony come morning. Whole town's in mourning. Not that we ain't had killings afore, but this is different. Bill was a highly respected citizen in his own right.'

'I heard about Bill Harding,' Mav ruminated. 'How come he got shot? Who gunned down on him?'

Skinny Billy was now in full flow. He described in graphic detail how Coyote Bill had struck out with his stock whip and snatched the Winchester from the sheriff's grasp and how Big Bravo had shot him down with his long-barrelled shooter before he had a chance to draw his side gun.

'Big man with a long-barrelled gun, you say?'

'Well over six foot tall,' Skinny Billy agreed. 'Sheriff could have drawn on him but the guy with the whip swept the Winchester right out of his hand before he could cock the danged thing.

That was real bad sas, that was.'

A man over six feet tall and a man with a whip: Mav certainly knew who they were.

'Clean through the head,' Skinny Billy concluded. 'I was right beside the sheriff too. Could have got shot myself. Felt the hot lead fanning past me the moment the big man shot him. 'Course, they patched him up good so's he looks in reasonable shape and peaceable as he lies in his coffin. Had a good conscience, Bill did. Best sheriff this town's had for many a long day. Fine coffin they made too. Bill Harding was a much respected and decent man.'

Mav nodded. 'Thanks for wising me up, old-timer,' he said. 'I'll tread real careful in case I injure people's feelings on that.'

He went in through the doorway and on into the lobby where the clerk was sitting behind his desk. Not so much sitting as drooping. He had had a particular liking for the dead sheriff. 'What can I do for you, sir?' He was eyeing Mav up and down trying to assess whether he might be another ill-doer come to town.

'Just dropped by to refresh my thirst.'

Somewhere within earshot he could hear the tinkling of a piano somewhat out of tune and the chirruping of female voices. It was a long time since he had heard such lively chirruping and chirping. It seemed that a few people in Cimarron weren't too distressed about the killing.

The clerk had raised himself slightly from behind his desk. He was watching Mav with evident curiosity. 'Ladies came in on the Butterfield stage,' he said. 'Probably on their way to California hoping to make their fortune in the acting profession.' He raised one quivering eyebrow. 'That where you're going to — California?'

'Could be.' Mav turned towards the room where he heard the more familiar clink of glasses. The barman wearing a long baize apron and fancy armbands gave him an enquiring glance. 'You

65

want whiskey, sir?'

'I'll take a glass of your best beer,' Mav said.

As the barman poured the beer, Mav surveyed the room and saw a woman with purple hair in full war paint and fancy clothes. This was Brassy Baby or the Queen of Sheba but he didn't know that.

He sat down at a small round table facing the door. Though he pretended not to notice, he saw the Queen of Sheba get up and drift over to his table. He noted that she was as tall as a man and possibly just as strong, which might be a disadvantage in her trade, unless, of course, you happened to meet Big Bravo.

'You just rode into town?' she asked needlessly. She had a quiet not unmelodious contralto voice. Most of the women in Mav's life had had high pitched soprano voices. So he was quite impressed.

'You drinking?' he asked.

'A girl always has a thirst,' she said,

batting her eyelashes. 'Mind if I sit down?'

'Be my guest.' Mav waved his hand over the table.

'So nice to meet a real gentleman,' Brassy Baby said in a mocking tone. 'I'll take a beer,' she added. 'Nice and cool.'

'Bring the lady a beer!' Mav called over to the barman. The man in the green baize apron ducked his head and drew a beer. 'That's as cool as it comes,' he said with a wink as he placed the foaming glass beside her on the table.

'You on the move?' Brassy Baby asked Mav.

'I might be, then I might not be,' Mav said evasively. 'I don't make big plans. They have a habit of going wrong.'

'Like the tumbleweed,' Brassy Baby said as she raised her glass and sipped her foaming beer.

Mav grinned and took a gulp of his drink. 'Wind blows you around somewhat. Never know where you're likely to wind up.'

'Well,' she said, winking with one of her heavily made up eyes, 'you don't look like a saddle bum to me.'

'Thank you, ma'am.' He raised his glass again. 'Could smell like roses after I've taken a dive into a bathtub and spruced up a bit.'

Brassy Baby's lips parted in what might once have been a Cupid smile. 'I could learn to like that.' She winked again.

Beneath the plastered make up Mav saw she had quite a bruise on her cheek. 'It might not be polite to mention it, but did you walk into a door or something?' he asked.

The painted face became more rigid and masklike suddenly. 'That bastard,' she said with loathing. 'Called himself Big Bravo. Beat up on me terrible bad. That's the man that killed Bill Harding. Bill was a particular friend of mine. He didn't deserve to die like that. Give me a shooter and I come face to face with that brutal bastard, I'll shoot him so many times he'll look like a busted pepper pot.'

Mav got up from the table. 'Well, I hope you get the chance to fulfil that promise and right soon,' he said.

'You going somewhere?' she asked. He saw in her eyes a look of something close to disappointment.

'Got business to attend to,' he said. 'I'll see you around. Buy yourself a real good dinner on me.' He took out several grubby dollar bills and laid them on the table.

The Queen of Sheba stared at the dollar bills in amazement. 'Is . . . is this some kind of insult?' she asked angrily.

'Don't take it that way,' Mav said. 'Maybe I'll catch up with you later. In the meantime, enjoy the best they have to offer in this establishment.'

Brassy Baby looked at the dollars again. Then she scooped them up and hid them between her breasts. The barman watching them from behind the bar pretended not to notice.

Mav gave him a cut-away salute and went over to the door.

Skinny Billy was rocking on his rocking-chair chewing a hunk of what looked like raw beef. 'You booked up to stay?' he crowed.

Mav glanced down at him meditatively. 'You mentioned the Widow Bean. Where does she hang out?'

Skinny Billy scrambled to his feet. 'Why, she's just along there a piece. White sign hangng down on one side like a buffalo sort of collided with it.' He regarded Mav in some amazement as he stepped down from the sidewalk and untethered Huck and the mule without a name.

Skinny Billy signalled to him from above. 'Didn't I tell you?' he said.

'Tell me what?'

'That Widow Bean is a somewhat of a witch. She could put a bad spell on you and turn you into stone like in those ancient tales.'

'That so?' Mav mounted up and patted Huck on the withers. As they moved away down the main drag to the place with the white sign where *a buffalo sort of collided with it*, the old geek scratched his head and said: 'Well, I'll be danged!'

* * *

The old man was right about one thing. The Widow Bean's place was leaning on one side like a drunk propping himself up against a telegraph pole. Outside there was a sign that said 'Rooms to Rent, Everything Included', but it was as dim as a winter's day in a storm. Just the place for a witch to reside, Mav thought. He couldn't make up his mind whether to dismount and thump on the door or turn around and ride back to the Cimarron Grand Hotel.

As he sat there considering matters, a big sheepdog came nosing around the corner of the building and raised its head. It was big and fierce but it looked kind of friendly.

'Looky here, Huck,' Mav said. 'Could be someone wants to welcome us.'

The dog gave a couple of quick yaps.

'There, Sheridan,' a woman's voice said.

Mav had expected someone different: an old crone with a chin full of whiskers riding on a broomstick. But this voice told a different story. The woman who appeared at the corner of the building was young. She had an apple-bright face and undaunted eyes. She was dressed in farm overalls and a farmer's cap and she was followed by a whole flock of clucking hens.

'Can I do something for you?' she asked somewhat abruptly.

Mav had removed his battered fedora. 'Just looking, ma'am. See you've got a sign up there, 'Rooms to Rent'.'

'Name's Letitia Bean,' she said, shading her eyes from the sun.

'That's a pretty name, ma'am,' Mav said.

'That's a damned awful name,' she rejoined. 'Means 'gladness' and I'm none too glad. What do you want? Did Colonel Dee send you over to harass me?'

Mav shook his head slowly and grinned. 'Don't know a Colonel Dee, ma'am. Just dropped into town. Man called Skinny Billy said you might rent out a room to me.'

Letty Bean gave a quiet laugh. Quiet but musical, Mav thought. 'Did old Skinny Billy mention I was a witch?'

'Come to think of it, he did use the word but I don't see a broomstick anywhere around so I think that might be an exaggeration.'

She shrugged. 'I keep it in the cupboard under the stairs.' She looked Huckleberry and the mule over and gave a nod. 'I see you treat your horses good. Take them to the stable round the back. My man Josh will look after them good. Then you can rest in the bathtub and have yourself a meal.'

'So you'll be renting a room to me?' Mav asked.

She gave him a long cool look and shrugged again. 'I guess you'll do.'

★ ★ ★

Mav figured Josh would be her husband but it turned out he was mahogany brown and he was some kind of do-it-all servant. He had a room adjoining the stable, but that was OK since he loved horses and spoke to them like a father.

'You set to stay long, master?' he asked in a deep friendly tone.

'I don't know how long I'm set to stay,' Mav said. 'Depends on a number of things, and, anyway, don't call me *master*.'

'What d'you like I should call you, boss?'

'I don't like *boss* either. Just call me Mav.'

Josh's sparse eyebrows shot up. 'That's a strange name, don't mind me saying so.'

'Short for Maverick, best name I've got. Born somewhere way back of beyond. They called me Maverick and that's stuck. So just call me Mav.'

'Yes, Mr Mav.'

The bathhouse was in an outbuilding. Josh heated up water in a boiler and filled the tub generously. He even offered to pour water over Mav's back, but Mav preferred to bide in the tub in peace for a while. So he lay back and Josh brought him a towel and a glass of rye.

'Miss Letitia says to tell you this is on the house,' Josh said.

Mav sat back in the tub and luxuriated, sipping his rye.

'Tell me, Josh,' he said. 'Who's the colonel?'

'You mean Colonel Dee, sir?' The eyes of the black man popped which said a lot. 'Guess you'll have to ask Miss Letty about that. None of my business. 'Cept to tell you Colonel Dee owns this whole town, more or less. Owns the bank too. They say the colonel is very rich and plumb mad about that bank robbery.'

'Not to mention the death of Sheriff Harding,' Mav speculated.

★ ★ ★

When Letitia Bean showed him to his room, he had a pleasant surprise. It was neat and tidy, the sheets were clean and white, and there was a bowl of prairie flowers by the window. A real woman's touch despite the farm overalls!

'You can come down just soon as you're ready,' she said. 'Good food in the pot. Guess you must be real hungry after that time in the tub.' She gave him a sly grin and left him alone to settle in.

When he went down all clean and dandy he found the parlour and the table set for two with Josh standing in the doorway dressed in a clean shirt, waiting to serve.

'A man of many parts,' Mav remarked.

'That's my job, Mr Mav.' Josh showed his good strong teeth in a smile. 'Miss Letitia does the cooking an' all. I just do the odd things around here.'

When the widow Bean came in she looked different, dressed in woman's attire with her hair caught up and tied with a black ribbon. Her dress was long and black, as though she was still in mourning for her husband.

'I come from the South-East,' she explained. 'Moved out here way back with my husband Mac and my . . . ' Her voice trailed away to a whisper and her lips puckered. She hid herself away behind a man's spotted kerchief.

'Good of you to take me in, ma'am,' Mav covered for her. 'Thought there might be other guests.'

'They come and go in all shapes and sizes.' She smiled. 'There's a Singer sewing machine salesman and two or three hardware salesmen. You never know exactly who might blow in.'

Though it was summer there was a cheerful log fire burning in the hearth and Sheridan, the German shepherd, was lying in prime position on the mat in front of it. When Mav entered the room he opened one eye and raised his head a little, then flopped down again.

'How old's the dog?' Mav asked.

'Oh, he's nearly twelve. Suffers from the rheumatics a bit but otherwise he's like an angel,' she said. 'Got him from an old lady who died two years back. Keeps me company.'

Josh delivered the pot of food in a very formal way like an old English butler. He had been trained well and obviously took his duties seriously.

'Food smells good,' Mav said, rubbing his hands together appreciatively. For a man who had lived on jerky and sardines dug out of a can so long this was no less than pure luxury. 'Looks like you keep up a good standard in this establishment.'

'Not for long,' she said. 'Place is falling down. I guess you must have noticed that. I had some hopes when I took it on two or three years back but I don't own the place and the lease runs out come fall. So the future looks dim.'

Mav glanced at Josh standing still as a statue carved out of mahogany but Josh betrayed no interest other than a slight blink of the eyes.

'Not like back in the old South-East,' Mav ventured. 'Life must have been a deal different in those days.'

She smiled ruefully and said nothing.

Mav nodded. 'You said you didn't care for your name, Letitia. Mind if I call you Gladness? That sounds more like you to me.'

Her eyes opened wide in surprise. 'That's what my husband called me.' For a moment Mav glimpsed the woman behind the mask of pretended heartiness: he saw something really sad lurking in her heart.

They ate for a while in silence. The food tasted even more than as good as it looked and smelled.

'You mind telling me about your husband Mac?' he said.

She shook her head and cleaned her mouth on her kerchief. 'Why d'you want to know that?'

'I just figured you were set to talk. It's none of my business. So maybe I should have kept my nose out of things.'

She was still shaking her head. 'No, that's OK. It's good to talk sometimes.' She paused for a moment as if bracing herself. 'Mac was a Scot, came from Glasgow or some place. We moved out to the New Mexico territory to find a new life. It sounded good and it was for a time.' She paused. 'We had two kids — daughters, Jemima and Prescilla, Jem and Prissy. Both cute little girls. I taught them at home, until that terrible day . . . ' She covered her forehead with her hand and held it there for while.

Mav put his knife and fork down beside his plate. 'You don't have to tell me. I see how painful this memory is.'

She raised her head and regarded him steadily. 'I want to tell you about it. I think you're a person who likes to listen and not just out of curiosity. I see it in you. So I want to tell you just what happened.'

And she told him.

★ ★ ★

They had established themselves close to the Sacramento Mountains in New

Mexico. At first it seemed something like heaven. Peaceful. No one around for miles. The ground was difficult to till and unforgiving, but they were making their modest way. Occasionally a lonesome traveller would drop by and stay a night or two. Mac enjoyed that. Despite being a dour Scot he liked to share a pipe with a stranger from time to time. Got on well with the Indians too . . . most of them. Navajos rode in to trade sometimes. Apaches too. Years before the Apache had been known for their gentleness and loyalty to their friends.

Then all that changed when they started raiding up from Mexico right up through the territory, killing and burning and sometimes raping. This was in 1877 when the troubles were at their height. Mac took it seriously, but not too seriously. He kept a loaded shotgun close by the bed and a handgun in a holster hanging from a peg in the living room.

'Those varmints won't come here,' he

said. 'We got a reputation for hospitality around here, Gladness. Apache don't bite their friends.'

But Geronimo and his band didn't know much about Mac's hospitality. They had had too many laws and restrictions pressed down upon them and they were mad with the whole white race.

It happened at dawn one morning. The sun was just peeping over the hill like a great yellow shining god when they rode in. Those renegade Apache were mostly young braves and they knew how to ride! No bones about it: those dog soldiers came for destruction and killing!

Mac and the two girls were out early working or toddling around in the patch. Gladness was in the cabin preparing breakfast. They always worked for an hour before breakfast. After the meal, the two girls did their reading and sums with their mother and Mac worked on until Gladness called him in for a frugal lunch. They never ate much until after sundown because of the hard discipline of the soil.

Mac had his shotgun standing against a post but he hesitated when he saw the dog soldiers. There were maybe twenty of them and they rode in silently. There was no shouting or war cries. Just silent dog soldiers riding in with their weapons raised. They were well-armed too, with newly minted Winchesters.

The two girls raised their young heads and stared. Jemmy, the elder and cleverer girl seemed to know instinctively what was about to happen. Prissy was squinting against the sun, wondering why these Apache men had come so early in the morning.

After a momentary pause, Mac reached out for his shotgun, just a bit too late. One of the Apache braves raised his Winchester and fired a shot. Mac fell back without so much as bringing his shotgun up to his shoulder. He had a hole in the middle of his forehead and he didn't even kick out with his legs.

Both girls ran screaming for the cabin.

Gladness had taken the Colt from its holster and she was at the door, running to protect her daughters.

Prissy stumbled and fell and attempted to rise.

One of the Apache men chopped right down on her with a tomahawk and sliced off most of her head.

Gladness raised the Colt with both hands and fired a shot. The Indian who had killed Prissy fell sideways and trailed off his horse. The horse reared and fell against the corral fence.

Jemmy ran to her mother screaming. 'Get behind me!' Gladness shouted as she fired shot after shot at the approaching Apaches. One fell, another leaped out of the saddle and pitched back bleeding. Gladness had practised well and she was a natural shot but there were too many Apaches to bring down. She had only two more shells left.

She turned, grabbed Jemmy by the hand and urged her to run. They ran together into the scrub behind the cabin.

Instead of running them down, the Apaches concentrated on looting the cabin. Now they were whooping and roaring and throwing things out in all directions. Then they shot the pig and killed the cow.

Gladness and Jemmy burrowed deep into scrub behind the cabin. Two shots, one for Jemmy and one for me, Gladness thought.

Then the cabin took fire and the Indians lost themselves in the excitement of the blaze. They were riding and dancing and hurling stuff on the blazing cabin.

Gladness experienced a moment of relief. Though her husband and one of her daughters were dead, she and Jemmy were safe. That was when Jemmy fell and started moaning. 'Momma, something hit me!' she cried.

How she had managed to run with

Gladness was past belief. She fell and died in Gladness's arms.

The cabin and the whole spread lay in ruins.

The Apache dog soldiers rode away whooping and roaring in triumph just as though they had won a great victory and deserved medals.

★   ★   ★

When Gladness finished her story Mav sat looking down at his empty bowl. She had told about the events and the destruction of her life in such an open and honest way without faltering or tears and he was deeply impressed.

Josh was still standing like a carved totem pole, but he suddenly came forward and stood beside Gladness as if to support her. 'You want for me to clear away the platters now, Miss Letitia?' he asked in a quiet and soothing tone.

Gladness nodded, rose quickly, and left the two men alone.

Mav and Josh exchanged glances. Josh gave a faint nod. 'That's a real sad story, Mr Mav.'

Mav nodded in agreement. Had Gladness hardened herself against the horror, or was she one of the bravest women he had ever encountered?

5

That night Mav made up his mind to stay on in Cimarron for a few more days, maybe as much as a week. Next morning he checked up on Huckleberry and the mule without a name.

'How you doing, old buddy?' he said to the horse. Huck tossed his head and got on with munching hay. He knew a good resting place when he found one.

'Hoss is doing fine, Mr Mav, sir,' Josh said from the doorway. 'Knows a good home when he sees one.' He grinned and showed his white teeth to Mav. 'You got a way with horses, sir. I see that right enough. A way with ladies too. Don't mind me saying so. Never heard Miss Letty spill out her sadness like that before. Not to me, not to nobody.'

'Can't figure why they call her a witch,' Mav said. 'She deserves a whole lot better than that.'

Josh paused for a second. 'That's because she has healing hands, Mr Mav. Docs don't like a woman with healing hands. So they spread bad rumours about them. That's how I come to be here in her service.'

'That so?' Mav said. 'How come you know about those healing hands?'

'Cos she healed me good when I had the croup. Couldn't stop coughing. Coughing so much I was fit to die, Mr Mav. Couldn't afford no doctor. Miss Letty made up some sort of medicine to drink. Cured me right off. That's why I do her service here.'

'Don't you have a family of your own?' Mav asked.

Josh furrowed his brow. 'Sure I got a family, Mr Mav. Way back in Louisiana. Wife and three young childer. I pray and hope I may see them again some day.'

'That's a good hope, Josh,' Mav said.

'Only trouble is,' Josh pondered, 'I'm stuck right here. Can't get back. Can't make my fortune. So I don't rightly know what to do.' He shrugged his shoulders. 'Not that I'm complaining none. Miss Letty treats me real good. But she can't stay here much longer neither. The colonel aims to shut down on the property. He has his own idea about how things should work out around here.'

'That must be Colonel Dee,' Mav said. 'I gather he's a hard man to please.'

Josh's eyebrows shot up again. 'I ain't saying nothing against Colonel Dee, Mr Mav. He owns the whole town, knows everything goes on here. He's real sore about the bank being robbed. They tell me he's offering a fat reward for those killers, dead or alive.'

'That so?' Mav said.

★　★　★

Later that day they were burying the late Sheriff Bill Harding up in the burying place on the hill. All morning the corpse lay in an open coffin receiving visitors. The undertaker and the doc had done a fine job patching him up so that a person could look down on his pale face without drawing back with horror.

It seemed the whole population of Cimarron was set to file past the coffin and pay their respects, comforting the widow and dropping in a flower or two.

Mav went along with the others as a matter of interest. The dead sheriff looked really peaceable lying there, and even Brassy Baby shed a tear or two looking down at his dead face.

'Never did a bad thing to nobody,' she murmured quietly.

'Couldn't guess he'd been shot down by a ruthless killer, could you?' a voice declared from close beside Mav.

When Mav turned he saw a man in a black suit, holding a black Stetson over his heart with respect. He was wearing a neatly trimmed moustache and no beard. You could say he looked as though he loved himself and looked after himself well.

The man gave Mav a keen glance. 'You must be the man called Maverick. Rode in yesterday, I believe. Staying at the Widow Bean's place.' All very businesslike. He stuck out a determined hand in Mav's direction.

Mav accepted the hand and felt its hard squeeze.

'I guess you must be Colonel Dee,' he said. 'Hear you own most of this town.'

Colonel Dee gave a deep and hearty laugh despite being so close to the dead sheriff. 'I don't claim to run it, but I do own a chunk of it,' he admitted.

'Including the bank and the widow's cabin,' Mav speculated.

The colonel gave him a look of close scrutiny. 'You are surprisingly well-informed for a man who rode into town just a day ago. How long do you intend to stay?'

Mav paused. He read irritation in the man's face despite his smile, but he saw that the colonel was a man of business who did not allow himself to be easily shaken. 'I like a man of perception. Why don't you drop by my office after the funeral and we can share a dram of rye together.'

'I might just do that,' Mav grinned.

Colonel Dee nodded. 'I might have a proposition to make. Could be a matter of profit for you.'

★　★　★

During the funeral Mav found himself standing next to Gladness. Though she had a kerchief close to her face, he noticed she didn't shed a tear. Control or hardness, he wondered?

They kept funerals short in those parts. The parson, who was also a part-time drunk, pronounced the words of the service in a fruity but brief manner as though he was anxious to get back to the few sheep he kept back of the parsonage.

'Nice service,' someone remarked as most of the towns-people flocked down from the burial place and in to the town.

'Saw you speaking to Colonel Dee,' Gladness said darkly.

'Invited me to take a drink with him. Said he might have a proposition to put before me,' Mav said.

Gladness was smiling secretly. ' 'Beware of barbarians bearing gifts',' she quoted.

'I don't accept anything that comes free,' he said.

He walked over to the colonel's office which you couldn't miss since it was in the most handsome building in town. Colonel Dee had been at the funeral with everyone else but had gone straight back to his office to get on with his many-sided business interests.

Mav tapped on the door and went right in with a smile at the young woman who stepped forward to admit him.

Colonel Dee was sitting behind a rather finely carved desk looking over some papers. He rose with the same steely glad smile that Mav had seen earlier. 'So you decided to come?' he said.

'Never could resist a good rye,' Mav conceded.

The colonel poured a generous measure for himself and another for Mav. He raised his tumbler and they clinked glasses together. 'Here's to good fortune,' the colonel said.

'Said you had a proposition to put before me,' Mav said.

Colonel Dee gave a faint nod. Then he sat back with his thumbs tucked into his vest and gave Mav a good hard look. 'I could have,' he said. 'First thing I see is you carry a gun. How good are you with that artillery?'

Mav surveyed him thoughtfully. 'Never thought about it. I have used it on occasion, but I don't practise much. A man needs a weapon when he's riding through the wilderness. Stands to reason.'

'You mean Indians?' Colonel Dee narrowed his eyes.

'Not so much,' Mav said. 'I'm no

Indian-hater. Indians I have encountered lately seem a deal more civilized than a few so-called white men I meet.'

Colonel Dee gave a calculated nod. 'You ever meet a big man with a special long-barrelled pistol name of Big Bravo?'

Mav gave a faint smile. 'Met him and his bunch on the trail. That was one good reason why I had my shooters. They were aiming to kill an Apache Indian but they had second thoughts about that.'

Colonel Dee nodded grimly. 'I guess you heard it was Big Bravo who shot down Sheriff Harding and robbed the bank. He and his sidekicks, four of them,' Colonel Dee said.

Mav considered a moment. 'The man who carries a stock whip is no sidekick,' he suggested. 'In my book he's the brains of the outfit.'

'That what you reckon?' the colonel said.

'That's what I figure,' Mav agreed. 'What's the deal?'

'Sheriff Harding was a good man. Now he's gone to the happy hunting ground this town is kind of stranded in terms of the law.'

Mav paused. 'That could be so, Colonel Dee.'

Colonel Dee was still sitting behind his desk. 'That means we need another lawman, I figure.'

'Could be,' Mav agreed again.

'You ever thought about taking to the law?'

Mav considered a moment. 'I don't think that's quite my style, Colonel. I have been called a saddle bum in my time, but I figure the title Sheriff wouldn't sit well with me.'

Colonel Dee nodded and smiled. 'You should think about that, Mr Mav. I could use a man like you. This town could use a man like you. I could deputize you right now while we're waiting on the judge. Might not turn you into a millionaire, but the money would keep you comfortable for a while.' He paused and drummed on his desk with his fingers. 'And I could do with someone like you by my side. That business with the bank was bad . . . bad for business . . . bad for everything around here.'

'I'll think upon that,' Mav said.

'You do that, Mr Mav,' the colonel said. 'Oh, and by the way I want the whole of that bunch of killers in dead or alive.'

'You mean Big Bravo and Coyote Ben and the rest of them?'

'Could be a reward in this, Mr Mav, for the right man.'

'What kind of reward?'

The colonel leaned forward. 'How does this sound? I'll give five hundred dollars for each of those killers dead or alive.'

Mav paused. Adding and subtracting had never been his strongest suits. 'I make that two thousand, five hundred dollars.'

'That sounds just about right,' the colonel said.

'Three thousand would sound a deal

better. One thousand for Big Bravo and one thousand for Coyote Bill. One thousand if we throw in the rest of the bunch.'

'That could be a good deal.' The colonel grinned.

'Well now, Colonel,' Mav put in after a moment's consideration, 'I don't rightly figure that. They robbed your bank and high tailed it. Your money's gone. You won't see it again. Why should you want those men killed. Is it for the good of the community or your revenge? I don't get it.'

The colonel grimaced behind his well-clipped moustache. 'Maybe a little of both,' he admitted. 'I figure you for a man with a good brain on his shoulders. Shall we just say I want those heads dished up on a platter.'

'Like John the Baptist in the Good Book,' Mav suggested. 'Now, Colonel, I don't want to sound too modest but I reckon you got the wrong man here. Sure, I carry a gun for my own protection, but I'm no gunfighter and no killer.'

Colonel Dee chuckled. 'That's the deal, Mr Mav. That and the job of sheriff. Could set you up real good.'

'Guess I'll need to put my hat on and think about that, Colonel.'

'You do that, Mr Mav.'

Mav walked out of the office and stood looking up and down Main Street. The town didn't amount to more than a row of beans. You could see to the end both right and left.

He had a lot to think about as he walked across to the Cimarron Grand Hotel.

* * *

Big Bravo was sitting by the fire in the woods. He was cleaning his shooter, looking at it thoughtfully and reloading it with shells. He didn't trust Coyote Ben any more than he trusted his dead aunt and he didn't trust the rest of the bunch either, especially Brokenwheel, who had the mean look of a man who never enjoys his food.

They had built a fire and Coyote Ben was sitting beside it with the gunny sack open. He had placed his shooter on the ground in front of him so he could grab it quick. He was counting the dollars they had taken from the bank in Cimarron. Rawhide was sitting close checking the dollar bills.

'Pretty slim takings,' Jim Sivers said. 'When do we get our cut?'

Coyote Ben looked up and eyed him closely. He had his back to a tree so that nobody could plug him through the head.

'You get it just as soon as we've counted it,' he said. 'Equal shares like we agreed, with a little off the top for me.' He grinned like an ape in the light from the fire.

Big Bravo was still loading his pistol. 'I don't recall that cut off the top. Anyways, who shot that stupid lawman?'

'You did it good,' Jim Sivers said in his high-sounding voice. 'Got him three times by my reckoning. That last shot through the head was classical, the way it jerked back like he'd been struck by a jack hammer.'

Big Bravo nodded with grim humour. 'Man who does the shooting gets the best reward. That's my reasoning.'

'Man who does the thinking gets the reward in my book,' Coyote Ben countered, ''specially if he carries a long snaky whip.'

The boys chuckled at that which didn't please Big Bravo none.

'I don't remember no thinking,' Brokenwheel declared. 'We all did our share of the thinking when we rode out with the loot. That's the way I reason.'

Rawhide and Jim Sivers shook with laughter.

Coyote Ben and Big Bravo eyed one another warily.

'What do we aim to do next?' Big Bravo said. 'Maybe we should go back into town and whoop it up.' He gave a gritty cackle of laughter.

'Sure,' Brokenwheel said. 'We just drift into town, shoot up the place, rest up in the Cimarron Grand Hotel and feed like gents for a while.'

'You off your tiny little head?' Rawhide said.

Jim Sivers sniggered again. 'Those floozies will be waiting with wide open arms and legs to welcome us.'

'I've got a better idea,' Coyote Ben said. 'I happened to notice the Butterfield stage leaves day after tomorrow headed along the Old Indian Trail towards Santa Fe. They carry gold on that coach once in a while. They stash it away under the driver's seat. Keeps him warm when the snows blow in.'

That caused laughter all round.

Big Bravo looked up suddenly. 'How do you know that about the Butterfield stage?'

Coyote Ben regarded him with a steady grin. Then he raised his index finger and tapped the side of his nose. 'I make it my business to know these things. That's why I'm the brains of this outfit.'

This time nobody in the bunch laughed. Jim Sivers and Brokenwheel exchanged sly glances and Rawhide gave a curt nod. 'Is this on the level, Coyote?'

Coyote Ben cocked an eye at him. 'Would I kid you on that? That floozie I spent the night with, she's got a sister works in the Butterfield office. We weren't playing all night, not like you boys. After I'd given her a few drinks, we got real friendly and she told me a few things. So I stored them up right here.' He tapped the side of his head with his middle finger. 'Didn't I tell you I have the brains.'

'So what do we do?' Big Bravo asked.

'We do the Butterfield stage, that's what we do. Then we share out the good dollars we get, and the gold, and we ride on to California some place, the land of dreams and angels. That's what we do.'

★　★　★

After the funeral Colonel Dee rode over to the house that Gladness occupied.

He tapped on the door and stood back to look at the place. Looks like its ready to fall down, he thought with a grin. When Josh opened the door and stood staring at him with ill-concealed amazement, he nodded briefly.

'Don't stand looking like an idiot,' the colonel said sharply. 'Go get your jaw oiled up and close your mouth. Then tell the mistress Colonel Dee's come visiting.'

'Yes, master.' Josh drew back goggle-eyed to let the colonel pass, but Colonel Dee swept him aside like a pile of garbage waiting to be collected in an alleyway.

'I take it Miss Letitia is in?' he enquired haughtily.

'Yes, master.' Josh watched the colonel's broad back as he strode on towards the parlour where Gladness was sitting patching an old pair of pants.

As the colonel appeared at the door, she stood up and let the pants slip to the floor. 'Ah, Colonel,' she said. 'Please come in and take a seat.'

Colonel Dee removed his black hat and surveyed the room. 'You keep things very nice here, Letitia,' he said. He held out a bunch of flowers he had brought. 'Perhaps you'd like to put these in a vase. Pretty the place up a bit.'

Gladness stared at the flowers in astonishment. 'Well certainly, Colonel. That's very kind of you. I wasn't expecting calls today, not after the funeral.'

'I guess not,' the colonel said brusquely. 'It's a sad time for the whole town. But I've been meaning to call and now seems to be as good a moment as any.' He placed his hat on the table and sat down.

'I guess you'd like some tea,' Gladness said. She was wearing her old farm woman's outfit but it didn't detract from her looks. In fact, the colonel thought it rather enhanced them.

'I came for a particular purpose,' the colonel announced ponderously.

Gladness had moved to the door. She was giving instructions to Josh about tea and teacakes. So the 'particular purpose' was momentarily lost on her.

The colonel fidgeted with the brim of his hat and thought the room was somewhat stuffy.

Gladness resumed her place at the table and picked up the pants she had been patching. She folded them up and put them beside the sewing machine.

'I been thinking,' the colonel resumed. 'I noticed as I came in, the place looks set to fall down and you know I can't afford to keep it on. Business is business and money is money. I think you'll agree to that.'

Gladness looked up slowly with sharp but wary eyes. 'Why don't you say it, Colonel Dee. You've come to throw me off the property.'

Colonel Dee gave her a slow look over. 'Now I didn't say that, Letitia. Fact is I came with something different in mind.'

'And what would that be, Colonel Dee?' She eyed him again cautiously.

'Well' — the colonel reached out for his hat again — 'I thought maybe you might consider the question of matrimony . . . '

The proposal fell on Gladness like a deluge of snow from a pine tree after a storm. She looked directly at the colonel with a mixture of astonishment and horror. 'Are you asking me to marry you, Colonel Dee?' she said.

Colonel Dee nodded. 'That's what I had in mind, Letitia.'

Gladness was inwardly amazed but she wasn't going to show it. 'I thought you already had a wife, Colonel,' she said.

That was a sore point with the colonel. 'I did once have a wife,' he admitted.

'And what happened to her, Colonel Dee?' she asked with uncanny directness.

The colonel fingered the brim of his black hat again. 'She left for California a year back. I haven't heard from her since. A year's long enough. I guess I'm free to marry again now.'

Gladness had known the colonel's wife. The poor woman had confided in her before she ran away in search of a better life. Rumour had it she had gone off with a gold prospector but nobody knew for certain.

Gladness shook her head and gave a wry smile. 'Is that what the law says?'

The colonel had started to boil. She could see that. He was a man who was used to getting his own way.

'Out here, the law doesn't mean much,' he growled. 'When a man loses his wife, he's free to get another. The same with a woman, I guess.'

Gladness nodded. 'There are two laws for me, Colonel, and I like to keep in line with both of them.'

Colonel Dee was still smiling, but behind the eyes she could see he was set to boil over.

'Thank you for your very kind offer,'

Gladness said tartly. 'I'll think it over and let you know later.'

The colonel got up from the table stiffly. 'End of the week,' he said harshly. 'I'll come back this day next week for my answer.'

He went to the door as Josh was about to enter with a pot of tea and some teacakes piled up on a plate. Josh had composed his face but his eyes were still goggling with astonishment.

The colonel almost collided with him. He gave a snort and raised his hand. Josh drew back and disappeared with the tray of teacakes.

The colonel stood in the doorway as though reflecting for a moment. Then he turned slowly. 'See you got a new man renting your spare room,' he said. 'You got two men in the house, one white and one black.'

'What are you saying, Colonel?' Gladness asked in surprise.

Colonel Dee gave an abrupt nod. 'A black serving-man is one thing but a paying white live-in guest is another.'

He spoke the words *live-in guest* with dark innuendo.

Gladness reached out and rang the bell on her table.

Josh appeared immediately without the tray.

'Show the colonel out, if you please,' Gladness said regally.

'Yes, Miss Letitia.'

Colonel Dee walked out fuming, but he hadn't finished yet. He turned in the hallway and, brushing Josh aside for the third time, came back into the room again.

'By the way,' he said with a kind of slow sneer. 'There's something I thought you ought to know.'

'What's that, Colonel?' she asked calmly.

Colonel Dee nodded confidently. 'That man you've got staying here as your live-in guest. Calls himself Maverick, I believe?'

'That's right.'

Colonel Dee nodded. 'Maverick,' he reflected. 'That's no name for a man, is it? More like a wild steer.'

'I guess that's what he wants to be,' she said.

The colonel was grinning. 'Your guess is good. Calls himself Maverick because he wants to hide his real God-given name.'

'Could be,' she agreed. 'That's no never mind to me.'

'Could be,' he said. 'Specially when I tell you his real God-given name is Bolder — Jesse Bolder.'

Gladness paused, looking for the punch line. 'Jesse Bolder. What's with Jesse Bolder?'

The colonel was now shaking with silent laughter. 'You don't read the papers do you, Mrs Bean? You read the papers you'd know who Jesse Bolder is. Wanted by the law back East. Tennessee, I believe. Price on his head ... ' He paused dramatically. 'Wanted for murder so the papers say.'

Colonel Dee saw the widow's mouth fall open. He chuckled quietly. 'The way I figure it, a lady in your position can't be too careful. People talk, you know.' He chuckled quietly to himself. 'Think over what I said, Mrs Bean.'

He turned and went out. She heard the door slam.

Josh was standing close by with a look of astonishment on his mahogany face.

6

Down at the Butterfield depot things were beginning to hum. They were loading up a special cargo. Nobody was sure what it was but Mav happened to be standing by and he saw men lifting a heavy box and stowing it away under the driver's seat. A tall man, name of Jake Osborne, was hanging around toting a Winchester. His close-set eyes were peering round under the brim of a sombrero-type hat and he looked mean. He was about to ride shotgun on the stage. When the driver, Hank Littlemore, who stood by him smoking a quirly, cracked some kind of joke, Jake Osborne twisted his mouth in a snarl that was meant to be a grin and spat a long stream of tobacco juice out on to Main Street. It almost reached the little group of travellers who were about to embark on the coach: two rather refined-looking women of uncertain age and two men somewhat haggard and drawn around the eyes.

'Who the hell are they?' Hank Littlemore joked. He knew full well who the passengers were. He had seen them laughing and joking and getting drunk in the Cimarron Grand Hotel where they had been staying for several nights on their way through from somewhere East. The man with the sunken features and who was most drawn round the eyes had proved himself to be a drinker of immense capacity. 'Must have hollow legs,' the booking clerk with the fancy vest had joked very quietly to Brassy Baby. He had booked the party into the big room that Big Bravo and Coyote Ben and the bunch had taken over the night before they robbed the bank and killed the sheriff.

'Band of wandering players,' Brassy Baby had said.

'What's a wandering player?' the man with the fancy vest had asked.

'That means actor,' Brassy Baby informed him. 'You know, actors act on the stage, pretend to be real people.'

'Heard about that,' one of the other girls said. 'You mean other people pay them money for that?' she squeaked.

'Sure,' Brassy Baby said knowingly. 'Some get plenty money. They have their names up in lights in New York and other places back East. That's why they drink so much. Can't make up their minds whether they're real people or imaginary people. They get confused.'

'Is that right?' the other girl marvelled. 'How come you know these things. Baby?'

'I been around.' Brassy Baby rolled her eyes.

'Didn't do no acting here in Cimarron,' a man said gloomily.

'Resting,' Brassy Baby explained. 'That's what actors do: rest up and drink before they go on to the next place. I hear they mean to go on to Santa Fe. Maybe folks in those parts have a taste for acting.'

Mav had been listening to the conversation in the Cimarron Grand Hotel. He knew that Brassy Baby had been trying to impress him with her knowledge of the theatre and its ways. Brassy Baby had ambition. He could see that. She didn't say much to him because she hadn't figured him yet but he noticed she glanced in his direction several times.

When they loaded up the Butterfield stage he was standing under the ramada watching. He saw Jake Osborne looking him over with suspicion from under the wide sombrero. He read Osborne's lips as he spoke to Hank Littlemore.

'Who's that shady-looking guy looking at us from over there?' Osborne said.

Hank Littlemore grinned and sucked on the stub of a quirly. 'Oh that's just some saddle bum drifted in a few days back. Staying with the witch. Doesn't say a lot. More or less keeps himself to himself. I figure he might be a wizard or something.'

Osborne shifted his hand on the Winchester. 'Don't know about wizard. Didn't he ride into town a couple of days after the sheriff got killed? Could be he's spying us out or something.'

Littlemore sniggered. 'If he'd been a spy he'd have come in before the robbery. Nothing to see after the robbery 'cept a dead sheriff. Stands to reason, don't it?'

'That may be so,' Osborne said, still glaring at Mav from under the brim of his sombrero. 'But I see he's packing a shooter. That must mean something, sure enough.'

'It just means he's a shootist of some kind,' Littlemore drawled. 'You get shootists on both sides of the law. Everyone knows that.' He flicked what was left of his flattened quirly into the dust and prepared to climb up into the driving seat.

A Humpty Dumpty figured appeared at the door of the Butterfield office. It was Stan Baldock, the Butterfield agent. He took out an oversized gold-plated timepiece and squinted at it through the minute glasses perched on the end of his nose. 'You all set, boys?' he said officiously.

'All set, Captain!' Hank Littlemore declared, giving him a cut away salute. He climbed somewhat creakily up on to the driver's seat and perched there, waiting while Stan Baldock bowed to the ladies and helped them on board.

Osborne took a last suspicious look at Mav and climbed up somewhat more nimbly to perch beside Littlemore.

One Winchester and one shotgun, Mav thought. Two clay pigeons waiting to be shot!

The two haggard actors, one of whom had a face as lined and riven as Abraham Lincoln's, got up into the cabin and Stan Baldock fastened the door elaborately. He could have had a stage career himself, Mav thought.

'Take it away, boys!' Stan Baldock slapped the side of the coach with his hand. Hank Littlemore cracked his whip. The stage drove out of town, accompanied by rousing cheers from the gathered townsfolk.

★ ★ ★

'What I can't figure,' a familiar voice said, 'is why you're still hanging around here, Mr Mav.' Mav turned slowly to look. It was Brassy Baby and she was addressing him. He didn't like that *Mr* attached to Mav. It made the name sound ridiculous.

'You don't need to figure it, Miss Brassy Baby, because it's none of your business.'

Instead of taking offence and bridling up, Brassy Baby just threw back her head and laughed like a man. She was dressed up and painted up as usual and laughing like a man didn't seem right.

'That's true,' she said. 'But I can't help thinking about it. I see a man looks a bit like a scarecrow riding into town with a shooter on his hip just after the sheriff has been shot and the bank has been robbed, and I put two and two together — '

'And make five and a half,' Mav prompted.

'It don't take a math graduate to work that one out,' Brassy Baby hooted.

'So what else did your busy brain work at?' he asked.

'My brain says this,' she said. 'This guy who looks like a scarecrow ain't nothing of the kind. After he's cleaned himself up and changed into clean dudes he begins to look more like a man — a man with ambition an' all.'

'Why, thank you for that kind thought.' Mav tipped what was left of his old fedora.

Brassy Baby was studying him closely. 'About time you invested in new headgear,' she said. 'Anyone can see that battered old headpiece is just a disguise. Get yourself something more dignified. Know what I mean?'

Mav was surprised. Out here on the frontier people didn't talk like that, especially painted ladies. You usually treated a stranger with silent suspicion.

'Anything else on your mind?' he asked.

'Oh there's a whole lot on my mind,' she declared. 'As I say, this *hombre* rides into town looking like a rat come in from the desert and he calls himself *Mav*, which is no name for a man. And, after taking a drink in the Cimarron Grand Hotel, he goes and lodges with the Witch.'

'That's OK,' Mav said. ''Cept that Mrs Bean is no witch.'

'Well, that's the way they say it,' Brassy Baby insisted. She shrugged her shoulders. 'Why don't you come up to the Cimarron Grand and settle in? I could give you a real good time. You're an ambitious man. I see that. I'm an ambitious woman. We could team up, go places together, you and me.' She fluttered her big fake eyelashes at him. 'Think about that and get yourself a neat headpiece.' She gave a high girlish crow of laughter.

'Thanks for the offer. I'll give it my full attention,' Mav said.

★　★　★

When he walked into the widow's house things seemed darker than usual. Not only the house, but the people. Even the hens in the yard, not to mention Sheridan, the big sheepdog; even he looked somewhat crestfallen in the jowls as he waddled up to Mav.

Josh, the servant man, was hovering around by the front door. When he saw Mav he came forward cautiously. 'Welcome, Mr Mav. I hope you're quite well today.' Josh looked down in the mouth like the dog and Mav figured it was more than a sheriff's funeral to account for it.

'What's wrong around here?' he asked.

Josh straightened up immediately and arranged his face to look happy. 'Why, there's nothing wrong exactly, Mr Mav. The horse and the mule are doing real good. I let them out in the field back of the house and they seem mighty pleased. Like heaven to them, I guess.'

He exposed his ultra white teeth in a grin.

'That's fine, Josh. You're treating those dumb beasts so well they won't want to go on the trail again.'

'Yes, Mr Mav, sir.'

'Where's Miss Letitia?' Mav asked.

'Oh, she out there on the back porch, Mr Mav, sir. She's thinking, sir. Set to figure things out. Mrs Bean's got a lot of things to figure, sir.'

Mav pushed open the screen and looked out. Gladness was sitting on a rocking-chair with an old paper spread out on her lap. She was wearing black widow's weeds and Mav figured she was grieving over her dead husband and those little girls the Apache Indians had killed. It takes a long time to get over grief like that.

He was about to duck back and close the screen but she looked up suddenly and saw him standing there just inside the house.

'Oh, Mav, why don't you come right

out here. I'll ask Josh to bring refreshments.'

'I don't want to disturb your thoughts, Gladness. I can see you're kinda down.'

Gladness shrugged her shoulders and didn't deny it. 'I'll be glad of your company here on the porch,' she said. 'You can help to brush away the dark shadows in my mind.' She smiled wryly.

Mav sat on the steps, half-turned towards her.

She was watching him with a kind of critical interest, yet he felt her sadness hovering in the air like a cloud between them.

'I see you're still wearing that gun of yours,' she remarked.

Mav shrugged. 'Matter of habit, I guess. Never managed to get properly house-trained.' He unstrapped his gun-belt and laid it beside him on the wooden floor. Somehow, it emphasized itself against the wood as though it had become a separate guest out there on the porch between them.

'Did you ever use that thing?' she asked.

Mav hesitated. 'I did have occasion to use it from time to time. Kept me out of one or two scrapes. That and the Winchester. Never know who you're going to meet in this wild country, do you, Gladness?' He turned to look at her and she was watching him keenly as though searching for some kind of clue to figuring him. Despite her pervading sadness, those eyes were bright and shining with intelligence.

'Not only in this wilderness country,' she half whispered. 'I mean back East.'

Back East, she had said. That gave Mav pause for thought. 'There's a hell of a lot back East,' he said. 'Did you have anything particular in mind?'

She paused for a moment. 'I'm not sure, Mav. Would you mind if I throw a name in your direction?'

He raised his head and their eyes met directly again. 'What name would that be, Gladness?'

Again she paused but her eyes didn't

waver an inch. 'Is the name of Jesse Bolder of interest to you?'

Mav didn't exactly flinch but he turned to look towards the pasture where Huckleberry and the mule without a name were grazing companionably.

'I'm Jesse Bolder,' he admitted. 'Maybe I should tell you about him, Mrs Bean.'

* * *

Jesse Bolder worked in a store in a town in Tennessee. He had worked there just over a year. Lived in a small rented apartment close to the railroad. The locomotives rattled through day and night and the apartment building shook like a drunken man set to wobble over and fall. Not the best place for a man to live. Certainly not the best place for a young man like Jesse.

Jesse lived there alone in that dank apartment in the shaky building. He got up every morning before light and walked across the railroad bridge and into town to The Big Sale Store, his place of work. He was doing well as a salesman in the store. The manager was pleased with him and wanted to promote him. One day Jesse would be a manager in his own right, but he had no hankering for that trade. His mind was elsewhere. Somewhere West maybe. He had heard a man could make his fortune in the goldfields of California and that was where his future seemed to point.

Jesse had moved out of the family place when his mother Sarah Bolder took up with another man called Bob Carvill. Jesse's mother was a widow. Her husband, Jesse's father, had died in a railroad accident. He had been with a team fixing the track. He was foreman and one of his men did slovenly work. One day Jesse senior bent over to check on a sleeper and a locomotive came chugging through the station. When it reached the place where they were working it was riding quiet and smooth.

The men in the team stood back and watched as Jesse senior bent forward to examine the track. Someone shouted a warning but it was too late. As Jesse senior tried to straighten up, the locomotive caught him sideways and took his head right off clean as a guillotine knife.

So, what was a widow woman to do?

That was when Bob Carvill showed up. Carvill was a giant who claimed to be descended from English royalty. He could talk like a king and drink like an English lord. Sarah met him one day in the market where he stood on a corner singing in a rich baritone voice.

'Good morning, pretty woman!' he said, doffing his imposing brown bowler.

Sarah's heart fluttered. She had never heard such a rich baritone, not even in the theatre. She was ensnared like a bird immediately.

They talked and walked together. He invited her to step inside the hotel just along the street and take a bite with him. Bob Carvill seemed the embodiment of all her dreams: big, strong-looking, with a rich voice and a sense of humour. When he laughed he set the whole street to laughing.

But that was only the good side. There was another side to Carvill. After he moved in with Sarah, the other side showed. Carvill had never done an honest day's work in his life. He would sit there in the house all dressed up, eating, drinking and telling tales of past adventures that existed only in his mind. He had the silver tongue of an Irish fortune-teller, but when he got drunk, which was more and more frequent, he became mean, morose, and violent.

Jesse Bolder was working hard at the store at the time. When Carvill moved in Jesse quickly took the measure of the man and decided to move out. He figured his mother deserved the chance to improve her life and he didn't intend to stand in her way.

That was before he realized that

Carvill was a sponger and a waster, and a leech. When he realized that, he began to visit more to make sure his mother wasn't being abused. Relations between Carvill and him deteriorated very quickly. The big man thought he could throw his weight around and he was quite heavy. When he was morose and drunk he took to beating the hell out of Sarah. She tried to pretend it wasn't happening, but one day Jesse walked in unexpectedly and found her crying with her head in her hands.

'What's the matter, Ma?'

She looked up like a pitiful clown with two black eyes and a streak of blood on her face.

'What happened?' Jesse asked.

'Nothing,' she said defensively.

'Nothing happened! What do you mean, nothing happened? Did that bully beat up on you, Ma?'

She shook her head, then glanced towards the door and burst into tears.

'Where is he now?' he asked her. 'Did he go out?'

She glanced towards the door again. 'You mean he's up there in bed?'

She nodded bravely. 'He went to sleep it off. It's nothing.'

'Nothing!' he repeated. 'Does this often happen?'

She made no reply.

Jesse got up and went to the door.

'Let it be,' she said.

'Let it be!' he raged. 'Sure, I'll let it be!'

Before she could stop him he went fuming upstairs. The door was open and he saw the huge palpitating form of Carvill lying face up on the bed, his mouth hanging grotesquely open.

Jesse went to the bed and glared down at the hulk. He might have just kicked him right out of bed and jumped on him a few times, but Carvill wasn't yet deeply gone and he opened his eyes in an alarmed stare.

'You beat up on my ma!' Jesse shouted. 'You damned rotting carcass, you beat up on my ma, you measly pig turd!'

132

Carvill jerked up in bed real quick, but not quick enough to avoid the fist that connected with his jaw. His head rocked back against the headboard and he rolled to one side to avoid a second blow. He was a big man and you might have expected him to be sluggish in his movements, but that fist had knocked the liquor out of him without putting him to sleep and he sprang up like a cornered mountain lion. He lashed out with one long arm and connected with Jesse's shoulder. But Jesse had taken boxing lessons to keep himself in trim and he ducked and sent out two quick blows to the man's guts. His fist sank right into Carvill's big paunch and sent him doubled and staggering right back to the window.

Jesse went after him, jabbing right, left, and right again. The big man fell against the window, went right through and disappeared with a yell. Lucky for him there was a bush that saved his fall. When Jesse looked out he saw Carvill spread-eagled and staring goggle-eyed like he couldn't figure whether it was a man or a steamroller that had hit him.

Jesse made to rush down the stairs and finish the job. He didn't know what he would do. He was still half-blind with rage, but he knew he would do something to that big blundering bear his mother had taken to her bed.

He met his mother at the bottom of the stairs. She had her hands to her mouth and she was screaming so loud the house seemed to rattle and shake.

'What have you done! What have you done!' she screamed.

'What have I done?' he shouted back. 'I kicked that bum right out of your life, that's what I've done.'

He grabbed the shotgun his mother kept behind the door and went out into the yard.

The bush was flattened but there was no sign of the hulk. The back gate was open and he had fled!

* * *

That was the end of the fight and almost the end of Carvill . . . but not quite.

When Jesse went into the house again, his mother was weeping and her streaming black eyes made her look even more like a pathetic clown.

'Ma, I've got to get you out of here!' he said.

She shook her head. 'I'm not leaving, not now, not ever. This is my home! What have you done? What have you done?'

'What have I done? I've thrown that beast from hell out of the house. That's what I've done.'

'You nearly killed him, that's what you did! He may be bad when he's drunk but he's trying to reform, and I'm helping him do that.'

Jesse didn't know what to do. His mind was in a whirl. Did his ma like being beaten up? He couldn't believe it. She had been such a strong, independent woman when his dad was alive. It seemed she had gone to pieces and he hadn't seen it.

He left the house and went to a saloon to think on things. He stayed there thinking until the bartender came over and cleaned off the table. 'You OK, bud?' he said.

'Sure I'm OK,' Jesse said angrily. 'Why wouldn't I be OK?'

The bartender held up his hands and backed off. 'Just thought you looked a bit drawn about the mouth. Nothing to worry about.'

He went back behind the bar and got on with his business.

It was at that moment that Jesse heard the fire department bell jangling. Not an unusual happening. But on this occasion, Jesse sat up and a feeling of dread shuddered right through his body.

He got up, grabbed his hat, and ran out of the bar. From the street he saw the plume of black smoke rising and the flames. That dread turned to a feeling of horror when he realized that the building on fire was his old home and that his ma was probably inside!

When he got close the fire crew were doing their best to quell the flames but the frame building was like an inferno. He rushed forward to beat his way inside but the heat hit him like a flaming fist and struck him to the ground. Next moment, as one of the fire crew dragged him back, the building went up in a huge explosion of flaming debris.

'My ma's in there!' he shouted. 'I have to save her!'

'No chance,' said the fireman. 'You'd get burned to a cinder!'

It took all night to put out the fire. All that time Jesse stood about in a frantic daze, hoping that, against all odds, his ma had been saved. Maybe she had run off and was hiding somewhere, trying to come to terms with what had happened?

When the fire was out the fire chief made a search. What was left of Jesse's ma was found crouching in the corner of the kitchen. She had been overcome by fumes and burned to death.

They found Carvill in the backyard later . . . or what was left of him. All his clothes and his hair were singed right off and his body lay close to the burned-out house. When they examined the body, they found he hadn't died from smoke inhalation or from the scorching flames. Someone had fired a shotgun at close range and peppered his torso full of holes.

★   ★   ★

'So that's what I have to tell you about Jesse Bolder,' Mav concluded.

Gladness had got up from her chair on the veranda. She was as pale as winter sunshine. 'Why, that's terrible!' she said. 'That's really terrible!'

Mav was still sitting on the top step with his gunbelt beside him. 'Aren't you going to ask me something?' he said.

She opened her mouth to speak, then closed it. 'That's a question I don't want to ask; I don't have the right to ask.'

Mav nodded towards her. 'You want to know who fired those shots,' he said.

Gladness made no reply. She was staring at him and waiting, the horror still in her eyes.

'Well,' he shrugged, 'you got to take my word for this. I didn't fire those shots. I don't know who did. Could have been my ma and it could have been someone else. When they found that shotgun in the yard it was so scorched and so burned there was no evidence.' Mav gave her a long look. 'You believe me, Gladness?'

Gladness didn't hesitate for more than a half second. 'I believe you. Of course I believe you.' She shook her head sadly.

Mav got up from the step. 'Well that's good, anyway.' He stood there with his gunbelt trailing from his hand. 'Nobody else believed me. The neighbours had heard the shouting and seen me busting Carvill out of that bedroom window. The police department drew their own conclusions. I guess they thought I had killed Carvill in a fit of rage and burned the house down and killed my ma. At my ma's funeral I saw them closing in and I figured they were set to pin the whole thing on me. That's why I decided to come West and start a new life.'

'Was that a wise decision?' she asked.

'No,' he said. 'It was a damned fool decision. I'm still trying to figure out the whole thing.'

'What's your conclusion?'

He thought about it for a moment. 'My guess is Carvill came back to the house, probably drunk, and he started the fire. An act of revenge that went too far. He was so full of booze and rage he didn't know what he was doing.'

'Then who shot Carvill?'

He shook his head. 'I don't know the answer to that. Could be some old enemy of Carvill's. There were plenty of them, men and women he had extorted money from and swindled one way or another. Could be a man or a woman. Shot him in the yard before the fire got a hold and before Carvill could escape.' He shook his head. 'Now I levelled with you on all that, I have to ask you something: how did you get to know about Jesse Bolder?'

Gladness considered for moment. 'Maybe I read about it in the newspapers,' she said.

'And something made you guess Jesse Bolder was the man calls himself Maverick.'

'Something like that,' she mumbled.

'Only thing is,' he said, 'I don't think you read the papers from back East. So what I figure is somebody else read that account and told you about it, and that somebody else had some reason to tell you those things.'

She flushed and turned away. 'I can't talk about that.'

'OK,' he agreed. 'We won't talk about it, but we don't need to. There's only one other person that might be . . . and it ain't Josh.'

7

High on the rocks west of Cimarron, Big Bravo, Coyote Ben, and the rest of the bunch were waiting. Rawhide was scanning the trail through a telescope where the Butterfield stage would come. Big Bravo was itching to move. He was fingering his long-barrelled Colt and tapping it against his knee like he was raring to use it.

'You see anything?' he enquired angrily.

'I see dust.' Rawhide squinted through his telescope. 'Looks like the stage is on its way.'

'Well, this is it, boys!' Coyote Ben said. 'This is where we get ourselves rich.'

'Yeah,' Big Bravo said. 'We get ourselves rich if that floozie said right.'

'Well, I'll take a bet on that,' Coyote Ben said. He held his whip across his saddle and drew his Colt. He spurred on his horse and led the way down among the rocks where they planned to intercept the stage.

'Maybe we should pull our bandannas over our faces,' Jim Sivers calculated. 'That way nobody will recognize us.'

'Like we did when we robbed the bank in Cimarron.' Rawhide laughed. 'When you held the horses,' he added mockingly.

'Don't matter much if there's nobody left to act as witness,' Brokenwheel said. He didn't smile. So you couldn't be sure when he had made a joke or when he was serious.

'Stop blabbering!' Coyote Ben said. 'Those people riding in the stage will hear you a mile away.'

Rawhide and Brokenwheel sniggered.

★   ★   ★

They needn't have worried about being heard. The group of actors in the stage were practising one of their stage songs, singing in not quite close harmony. The man with the face like Abraham Lincoln was conducting in lugubrious fashion and the other actor was dealing out a deck of cards on the seat opposite, beside one of the actresses.

Outside, seated side by side, Hank Littlemore and Jake Osborne hadn't said much so far. Hank Littlemore was marvelling at the rank childishness of actors and Jake Osborne had his big sombrero pulled down well over his eyes. Hank Littlemore was chewing sourly on a hunk of tobacco and he spoke from the corner of his mouth.

'I don't figure that bunch,' he said. 'I could sing a lot better myself if I had a mind to it.'

'Don't bother,' Osborne advised. 'One choir's enough for one day. I just hope we don't have to listen to this all the way to Santa Fe. 'Taint reasonable.'

Littlemore was just thinking up a suitable reply when he saw Big Bravo and the rest emerging from behind a rock.

'This looks like trouble,' he said, reaching down for his shooter.

'Sure does.' Osborne cocked his Winchester and held it ready across his body.

Coyote Ben rode out in front of the bunch and held up his hand. 'You boys like to stop the coach?' he said.

Osborne saw the stock whip looped across his saddle and his eyes turned to Big Bravo. He recognized him from the description of the *hombre* who had killed the sheriff.

The stage was already down to an amble. Had to be since the five gunmen were spread out across the trail. Osborne thought quickly and reasoned about his responsibility. He had to protect the passengers and the box sitting under the driver's seat. On the other hand he was in no mood to suffer martyrdom.

'Can't stop for no man,' he drawled. 'It ain't in the goddamn contract.' As he spoke he brought the Winchester round in the general direction of the robbers.

'Well, that's a pity about the contract because we don't give a damn,' Big Bravo said.

Littlemore had stopped chewing. He opened his mouth with the plug of tobacco jammed in the corner. He wanted to spit it out but it didn't seem the right moment.

The actors inside the coach had stopped singing. The Abe Lincoln lookalike stuck his head out of the window and saw Coyote Ben pointing a carbine in his direction.

'Anything I can do for you gentlemen?' he asked in a high, superior-sounding tone.

'Sure,' Brokenwheel crowed. 'You can shut your damned mouth before I put a bullet through your head.'

The actor's mouth opened wide and his head popped back into the coach so quickly the man with the playing cards spilled them all over the floor and the two women got ready to scream.

'Now, calm down, ladies,' the Abe Lincoln lookalike said. 'This is probably some kind of a joke.'

Next second they heard the crack of gunfire and knew this was no joking matter. Jake Osborne had brought his carbine into play a second too late. Brokenwheel had fired at him and lifted him clean off the seat. Osborne slid over the edge of the stage and plunged on to the ground with blood streaming from his mouth. He made no move to get up because, before he hit the ground, he was stone cold dead.

Inside the coach the two women started to scream. The card player got down on the floor to make himself as small as possible and the Abe Lincoln lookalike threw his arms about and tried to draw a small Smith & Wesson he carried in case of emergencies.

Hank Littlemore was no coward. He spat out his plug of tobacco and whipped up the team. The lead horses were spooked and jumpy. They sprang forward and galloped straight into the gang of robbers, causing them to draw back right and left.

Coyote Ben struck with his stock whip. It came snaking out and cracked against the driver's face. Littlemore lost the reins and clasped his right eye. He screamed with agony just as Jim Sivers sprang up beside him and pistol whipped him neatly across the side of the head.

Then the horses went into a gallop. The stage rocked like a ship on a wild sea. Sivers elbowed Littlemore out of his seat and scrabbled for the reins.

Those horses were truly spooked. They galloped on like demons with fire in their tails. The women screamed and the Abe Lincoln lookalike, whose stage name was Humphrey Henry, crouched behind the window and started blazing away with his Smith & Wesson. His third shot caught Rawhide who was riding close trying to claw at the window. Rawhide jerked out of the saddle and fell away behind his horse as though he was riding Indian style, keeping the horse between him and the coach. Next second he was lying in the sand with a hole in his chest just above the heart. His horse galloped on and then sheered away to the left.

Brokenwheel was riding ahead. He leaped from his horse onto the lead horse's back and struggled to bring the whole rig to a stop. The wheels bit into the dust of the trail and everything slithered to a grinding halt.

The two women had stopped screaming now. They were too busy holding themselves together in the slithering coach.

Next thing, Big Bravo jerked open the door of the coach and fired two shots at the Abe Lincoln lookalike, who recoiled against his seat and slumped down against the other actor, Job Basnett, who was busy trying to get his hands in the air.

'Don't shoot!' he pleaded.

Big Bravo gestured with his Colt. 'You ladies mind stepping out of the coach?' he said. He drew back and showed the way with his gun. The two actresses got out of the coach with some difficulty, they were shaking and gasping so much. Job Basnett scrambled past the inert body of Humphrey Henry and almost fell down behind the ladies.

'You killed Humphrey,' the taller of the ladies accused. Her name was Sadie Solomon and, despite her made-up appearance, she had a lot of grit.

'We didn't aim to kill anybody,' another voice declared. It was Coyote Ben and the two actresses saw at once that he was well-shaved and smooth, like a man who took care of his appearance.

'You killed him!' Sadie accused again.

Big Bravo gestured with his long-barrelled Colt but Coyote Ben brushed it aside and grinned at the ladies. 'We don't aim to kill,' he declared. 'Only in self-defence. When a man shoots at you, you have to shoot back. That's a matter of common sense. I think you'll agree.'

Job Basnett had scrambled up on to his feet. He was scared but his mind was clear. He saw that four men had died in the same number of minutes. Back on the trail the bodies lay in grotesque postures, Jake Osborne staring sightlessly at the sky and Rawhide turned over as though searching for something at his side. The body of Hank Littlemore drooped down from his driver's seat as if he had fallen asleep with his arms flung out wide.

Inside the coach Humphrey Henry was slumped against the seat with blood dripping from his head. No more Shakespeare or vaudeville for him!

'What are you going to do?' Sadie Solomon asked the question nobody wanted to utter.

Coyote Ben shook his head. 'What we're going to do, ma'am, is no never mind to you. There's been enough bloodshed already. That's a matter of regret. But all is said to be fair in love and war, you know.'

Big Bravo didn't want to know about love and war. He looked the two women over with lustful eyes and moved away to the front of the stage where Jim Sivers was struggling to get the box of loot clear. Big Bravo climbed up and pulled the body of Hank Littlemore free so that it fell in a grotesque heap on the trail.

'Careful with that stiff!' Sivers laughed. 'Don't want to bust it up so bad it won't be in any fit state to drive that big heavenly coach beyond the clouds.'

Big Bravo gave a hoot of derisory laughter and jerked the box free. Sivers slid it out from under the driver's seat and passed it down with due reverence to Big Bravo's eagerly outstretched hands.

'Feel like taking a walk, ladies?' Coyote Ben asked the two actresses.

'All the way to Santa Fe,' Big Bravo hooted. 'Or maybe you should come along with us, home comforts on the trail.'

★ ★ ★

Way up above the trail on the side of the hill, a pair of eagle eyes was

152

watching. They saw the stage and all that happened when Coyote Ben, Big Bravo and the others held it up. The owner of those eyes heard the shots and saw the puffs of grey-green smoke caught up on the breeze. He saw the horses drag the coach along the trail and come to an abrupt halt.

Now he saw Brokenwheel drag three bodies to the edge of the trail and lay them side by side, as if he was a funeral director. Then he saw Big Bravo and Jim Sivers try to bust open the box they had taken from the stage. After that he saw the two women who had been made to disembark from the stage hoisted up on horses that had been cut loose from the stage. Then heard the crack of a whip and saw Coyote Ben lashing out at the only man who had climbed free of the stage. Under the lash of that vicious whip the actor Joe Basnett had run for his life in panic. He had hopped, stumbled and sprawled. He scrambled to his feet and made off as fast as he could towards the rocks where he thought he'd be safe.

The man with the eagle eyes even heard high-pitched laughter as the four remaining robbers secured the box of loot up on to one of the stage horses. Then they mounted up and rode away, taking the two women with them.

★ ★ ★

Jim Sivers and Brokenwheel were riding one each side of the two actresses. Big Bravo and Coyote Ben were just behind.

'That was a damned fool thing, bringing those women along,' Coyote Ben said. Though he was a smart dude who liked to keep himself spruced up he had a deal of savvy.

Big Bravo looked down on him from high in his saddle. 'Like I said, home comforts,' he spat out from the corner of his mouth. 'One for me and one for you.'

'What about Jim Sivers and Broken-wheel?' Coyote Ben asked.

Big Bravo chuckled harshly. 'They can take their turn. By my reckoning, Jim Sivers ain't exactly one for the ladies. He should have been one of those fat monks in a convent or something.' He sniggered. 'Anyways, we got the box of goodies, don't we?'

'Yeah, we got the box,' Coyote Ben agreed sourly. Though he was pleased about the greenbacks and the gold coins in the box, he was still half thinking about Rawhide lying stiff beside the trail. 'I'm not sure I cared for the way Brokenwheel laid those bodies out side by side,' he added.

'I thought that was real neat,' Big Bravo said with a laugh. 'Looked kinda tidy and respectable, you know.'

'Looked more like a challenge to me,' Coyote Ben said. 'Four bodies lying side by side on the side of the trail, that could spell the worst kind of trouble. Some folk might figure it was a challenge that meant, I want you to come looking. We're going to shoot you just like we shot these stiffs.'

Big Bravo was nodding and laughing. 'They can come if they like. By the time they catch up on us we'll be living it up in California or some place like retired preachers or distinguished bankers.'

Coyote Ben gave a sceptical shake of his head.

Riding on, Jim Sivers and Brokenwheel were talking across the two actresses.

'Pity about Rawhide,' Brokenwheel said.

Jim Sivers twisted his mouth in a grin. He had never cared for Rawhide, thought he was a damned sight too clever at riling him up. 'I just hope he had time to say his prayers before he dropped.' He paused a moment to reflect. 'Leastways, we get a bigger cut that way.'

Brokenwheel had to agree with that. He glanced at Sadie Solomon and saw she was riding the stagecoach horse with a grim, determined expression on her face. He figured she might play a real heroine in any play she was in.

Jim Sivers was looking the other actress over. She was fairer and looked somewhat more delicate. Her professional name was Phoebe French.

'You been in the acting profession long?' he asked.

'Long enough to smell a skunk,' she said drily. 'Where are you taking us?' she added.

Jim Sivers glanced across at Brokenwheel. He wasn't sure of the answer to that question.

Sadie Solomon gave Brokenwheel a sideways glance. 'You know that big man back there killed one of the best actors in the Western world?' she said.

'That so?' Brokenwheel replied. 'Pity he reached for that Smith & Wesson. Must have thought he was a hero in a play or something. His last performance, eh?' He threw that across the women to Jim Sivers who gave a yap of laughter.

'Managed to shoot down Rawhide,' he rejoined. 'Kind of eye for an eye, you know?'

Sadie Solomon pulled a wry face. 'Worse thing you could have done, forcing us to ride along with you like this. People back in Cimarron won't care for that.'

'Which people?' Jim Sivers asked. 'That sheriff don't give a damn. He's stiff and dead in the earth.'

'There may be others,' Sadie said.

'Which others had you in mind?' Brokenwheel asked derisively.

Sadie sifted through the other characters she had seen in Cimarron. She remembered the man who had been standing there under the ramada, waiting for the stage to leave. 'Well,' she said, 'There's a man calls himself Maverick. Wears a battered fedora, packs a gun so close you might think he slept with it under his pillow nights. There's a rumour they offered him the sheriff's star after the sheriff died.'

Brokenwheel looked across at Jim Sivers suspiciously. No need to jog his memory on that one. Both of them remembered the incident with the

Apache Indian boy immediately. Jim Sivers gave a murmur of laughter. 'That scarecrow *hombre* has it coming to him. Sooner the better.' Though he spoke up boastfully there was something about the man called Maverick that gave him a shiver of apprehension.

Sadie Solomon noted his reaction and it quietened her fears somewhat. She glanced at Phoebe French and her expression said: keep quiet and pretend. We don't want these monkeys to know about the derringers we've got tucked under our bodices.

She gave a little inward sigh, regretting Humphrey Henry who had given them those derringers in case of emergencies. And this was one big emergency.

★ ★ ★

The actor Joe Basnett cowered behind the rocks for a while. Couldn't understand why those desperadoes hadn't pursued him and finished him off. He was a bad actor and a cowardly man. But like most people in the theatre he had a strong instinct for survival.

When he was sure the bandits had ridden away with the two women, he crawled out from behind a rock and peered about like a short-sighted gopher. He knew he had to think and act before he sank into a decline and died of helpless shock. At first he avoided looking at the corpses lying alongside the trail. But Humphrey Henry and he had been friends and partners for a number of years. He acknowledged that Humphrey was the better actor. Humphrey took the lead in both senses. Rumour had it he had played Hamlet once in a small theatre in Baltimore or some place. He was impulsive but brave. That was why he had gone for the Smith & Wesson, to his cost.

Joe Basnett forced himself to go over and take a look at his friend. Humphrey looked eerily calm, staring sightlessly up at the sun as though he was taking a rest after lunch in the open, except for the blood on his shirt front. Joe Basnett knelt down beside him and mumbled some kind of prayer.

'Listen, buddy,' he muttered. 'I want to thank you for helping me along the way. Without you I would have been nothing. And those killers won't get away with these murders. They'll get what's coming to them.'

He scrambled up from his knees and looked up at the hills. He thought of those two women being carried off by those desperadoes. 'By God, I have to rescue Sadie and Phoebe,' he said aloud. 'I got to save myself so I can rescue them.'

He looked round desperately and saw the stage not too far away without horses to pull it. He staggered over and yanked the door open. He saw his cards scattered over the floor and Humphrey Henry's spilled blood on the seat. He saw Humphrey's Smith & Wesson on the floor. Basnett hated weapons of any type but he leaned forward and picked up the revolver.

As he turned, clutching the weapon, he looked up and saw the figure of a man on horseback looking down at him.

★ ★ ★

Mav was out in the paddock talking to Huck. 'You know what it is?' he said quietly. 'I'm getting a damned sight too comfortable here. Maybe it's time to move out, go to California like we planned.' He ran his hand down Huck's neck and patted him like a beloved son. 'What do you think, my good boy?'

Huckleberry flung his head up to shake off a troublesome fly and gave his master a brief glance. You can always tell a horse's nature by its eye. Huck had a mild trusting nature. That was why Mav treated him like a son. On this occasion Huck didn't have much to offer in reply to the question. He had settled down well at the witch's place and he was happy to stay . . . maybe as long as for ever.

Mav patted him on the shoulder and turned to the mule without a name. 'What do you think, Mule? Do we stay or do we push on to California? It's a comfortable kind of deal here.'

The mule flexed back its ears and let out a huge braying noise.

'You said it, boy!' Mav agreed.

'I think you could give that beast a name, Mr Mav. Every critter should have a name. Stands to reason, Mr Mav, and that mule is almost human.'

Mav turned and saw Josh standing by the edge of the paddock. He was smiling wide and chuckling. 'Heard you talking to those dumb beasts, Mr Mav. I appreciate a man who knows how to talk to mules and horses. Shows a deal of respect for Mother Nature and all her critters.'

'That has some truth to it,' Mav agreed.

'Don't mind me asking, Mr Mav,

d'you aim to stay here long?'

'What do you think, Josh?'

Josh shrugged his shoulders. 'That's hardly my business, Mr Mav. I figure you for a man who likes to move on.'

'Like smoke, you mean?'

'Something like smoke. That's a good way of saying it. Smoke drifts. You can't pin it down to nowhere.'

'Unless you put out the fire,' Mav said.

That mutual philosophizing went no further. Gladness came out on to the porch and called to them. 'You hear what happened?' she said.

The two men walked over to meet her.

'What happened?' Mav asked her.

'From what I gather, someone robbed the Butterfield stage,' she said. 'One of those actors just rode in on an Indian pony. They say he's half-dead with fear and the ride. Stan Baldock, the Butterfield agent, is questioning him right now. He talks of killings. One of the actors and the driver and

164

Osborne, the man riding shotgun was killed.'

★　★　★

Mav walked down to the Butterfield depot and saw the Humpty Dumpty figure of Stan Baldock standing out on the sidewalk, looking anxiously up and down as if he was expecting an urgent message. The door of the depot stood open and several people were crowded inside.

When Baldock saw Mav coming down the main drag towards him, he drew back as though he was about to be assaulted.

'You hear what happened?' he gasped. 'They held up the stage. Shot Littlemore and Osborne and one of those actors. This is a bad tragedy for the stage line and for everyone in this town. Stole the strongbox too.'

Mav half-listened to him as Baldock blustered on. He was looking over the Indian pony tethered to the hitching rail. No mistaking it.

'That mustang,' Baldock said. 'That's what the man rode in on.'

Mav climbed the step and walked across the sidewalk. He was about to enter the depot when Brassy Baby came out. She was dressed less garishly than usual and she hadn't had time to put on much war paint. So she looked more human than usual.

'Did you hear what happened?' she said.

'I heard.' Mav looked past her and saw a knot of people standing around trying to question the man half-lying on a chair with a face as pale as curd. Among them Colonel Dee was wagging his head and listening. The actor Joe Basnett was spilling it all out. Mav caught the words, 'my best friend . . . and those two lovely women taken off by a bunch of cruel ravishers . . . '

Brassy Baby was twisting her fingers in the sleeve of her blouse. She was a fine-looking woman without her war paint, a fact that Mav hadn't taken much account of before. 'This thing is terrible,' she said. 'Makes you fit to cry.' In fact he could see by the streaks on her cheeks that she had been shedding tears. Brassy Baby wasn't as brassy as they pretended.

'Did you see him ride in?' he asked, inspecting the Indian mustang.

'I was standing outside the Cimarron Grand and I saw them riding, Joe Basnett and an Indian. The Indian didn't ride into the town. He just kept his distance and watched while Basnett rode on.' She paused to give Mav a keen and anxious look. 'You know those killers beat up on Basnett with that stock whip.'

Mav narrowed his eyes. 'Coyote Ben,' he said.

'That's the man,' she said. 'Gave that actor big weals right across his back, laughing when he did it too! Doc Tatum is with him now, treating those cruel wounds.'

Mav nodded and went on into the depot. Joe Basnett had stripped off his shirt and Doc Tatum was dabbing away with some kind of wicked-looking balm or possibly raw whiskey.

Colonel Dee glanced Mav's way and nodded. 'You see why we have to stop those killers?' he said. 'Did you think about my offer?'

'Sure, I thought about it,' Mav said. 'I've thought about a lot of things since our last meeting.'

Colonel Dee didn't take him up on that. 'At least they killed one of those ornery desperadoes,' he said.

'By my reckoning that makes four to go. We agreed on the price, remember: a straight three thousand dollars.'

Colonel Dee stroked his little tooth-brush moustache. 'I thought we agreed on five hundred for each man.'

Mav looked down Main Street in the direction Joe Basnett and the Indian had ridden.

'A straight three thousand dollars,' he said. 'That's to clear out the whole bunch.'

The colonel's eyebrows popped up.

'There's one down already; that makes four.'

'A straight three thousand,' Mav said. He gave the colonel a look of keen scrutiny. 'Leastways, that's what my close acquaintance Jesse Bolder tells me.'

8

Jim Sivers had kindled a fire and the whole bunch were sitting around it. The horses including the stagecoach horses, were hobbled close by feeding on what they could graze under the scrubby trees. Coyote Ben had chosen a good spot where they could rest up and spend the night. Sivers was rustling up some chow. He was a plain cook. They called him *bean master* as it was mostly beans and bacon and occasional jerky or pemmican or, occasionally, a can of sardines.

Sadie Solomon and Phoebe French were huddled together for mutual protection. They had their wrists tied behind them but Jim Sivers had done a sloppy job. So Sadie was already starting to wriggle her hands free.

The men (Phoebe would have called them *desperadoes*) were sitting by the fire. Big Bravo had lugged the strong-box off the back of the horse that was carrying it. He hefted it over to the fire and laid it down with the promise of great riches. 'This is our big day!' he roared! 'This is where our fortunes change and we get rich.' He gave a huge guffaw of laughter and struck the lock with a chunk of rock . . . with little effect. The rock broke in two and fell on the dry ground.

'Don't be in too much of hurry!' Coyote Ben advised. 'I guess we're all tuckered out. We should eat our chow, take a drink, and rest up for a while. What d'you think, boys?'

Jim Sivers and Brokenwheel murmured their approval. Brokenwheel couldn't make up his mind. Half of his thoughts were on the food and the booze. The other half were on those two handsome actresses squatting down by the fire. Which one would he choose? he wondered, Sadie or Phoebe? But his mind was split three ways and the thought of that treasure in the strongbox appealed to him more than anything. He glanced at Jim Sivers and knew he was thinking the same thing: we get the drop on Big Bravo and Coyote Ben we could be made for life!

Big Bravo could be an easy ride if you chose the right moment. You just shoot him right through the head when he's drinking his booze. He don't have time to draw that long barrelled shooter of his. Pow! Pow! End of story. Except we still have Coyote Ben to consider and he has a lot of savvy and eyes in the back of his head.

That was the way Brokenwheel figured it.

Jim Sivers was thinking on similar lines. He figured he might free those two actresses, get some kind of reward as well as the treasure in the strongbox. He had his eye on Phoebe French. She was softer than Sadie Solomons, reminded him of a woman he had seen in a play once a long time back. That was why he had tied those bonds so loosely. Maybe he could get those women out of there and gain some credit for it.

Big Bravo had drawn his Colt and was about to blast open the strongbox.

'Hold on!' Coyote Ben said. 'We know what's in there, don't we? We break open the box everything spills out and we can't carry it so easy.'

Big Bravo paused for a second, then roared with laughter again. The two women trying to make themselves look small didn't like the sound of that laughter. It had a cruel streak in it that made them shiver!

We might have to use our derringers, Sadie thought. Anything's better than being ravished by these beasts! She made a sign to Phoebe who appeared to be shaking away to nothing. 'Keep yourself together, baby,' she whispered. 'We might have to use our derringers but remember we only have one chance. So you can't afford to miss.'

Despite her shaking Phoebe nodded. 'D'you think they mean to harm us?'

Sadie smiled grimly. She knew they would be harmed. The way she figured it, she had to pretend to play along with these killers until the opportunity came, but would Phoebe be strong enough to move when the time came? She was a passably good actress but had she the brains and the stamina to hold on?

'Time to feed!' Jim Sivers shouted. 'Step this way, gentlemen, so I can load your platters up!'

Brokenwheel went forward eagerly, but Big Bravo pushed him none too playfully aside and seized his tin plate first.

Coyote Ben seemed to be in no great hurry. He was breaking out a bottle of rye he had been keeping to celebrate. He yanked out the cork and spat it into the fire. Then he took a swig from the bottle and nodded.

Watching him, Sadie thought: He's the most dangerous of the bunch, he has some kind of plan of his own.

Having served the other two, Jim Sivers loaded a platter and took it over to Coyote Ben. 'Here's your chow,' he said almost reverently. Coyote Ben tucked the bottle between his boots and took the platter. 'Why, thank you Jim. That's really kindly of ye.' He grinned.

Sivers moved over to the two women. 'You want feeding, I guess?'

'We're as hungry as you,' Sadie said, giving him a kind of half-smile. 'Trouble is we can't eat properly unless you untie our hands.'

Jim Sivers grinned and showed a row of uneven teeth. 'Why sure', he said. 'That's no problem. Must keep the womenfolk happy, don't we?'

As he untied their bonds from behind, Sadie looked across at Phoebe and gave her a wink. Phoebe made a slight inclination of the head to show she understood.

Sivers went to the fire and loaded two tin platters with food. He brought them over to Sadie and Phoebe and laid them almost gently in their laps.

'You're gonna be safe,' he whispered to Phoebe. 'That I promise you.'

Coyote Ben was passing round the bottle and Big Bravo and Brokenwheel were swigging back whiskey as though the end of the world was nigh. It went down well with bacon and beans! The first bottle was almost empty but Coyote Ben had another stowed in his saddle-bag and he opened it with relish.

He's not drinking much, Sadie noticed. Wants to get the others drunk. I guess this might be the moment of truth.

The meal was over. Jim Sivers collected the empty plates and wiped them off with a bunch of leaves. He stowed them away in a saddle-bag just as Big Bravo lumbered up and drew his shooter again.

'Now we have to break open the strongbox and have ourselves a share out,' he declared.

'Hold on there,' Coyote Ben said. 'That box is heavy and awkward. Maybe we should keep it good.'

Big Bravo swaggered over to him. 'I don't go with that!' he said. 'I'm gonna blast that can open right now!' He turned and fired at the lock on the strongbox. The bullet ricocheted off with a whine and lodged itself in a tree close by, causing a shower of debris to come down. The hasp hung broken but there was a big dent in the strongbox.

'Now that's gonna be dang difficult to open!' Brokenwheel groaned.

'That ain't so difficult!' Big Bravo said. He stepped back and fired another shot at the lock. This time the bullet rebounded from the strongbox and twanged off close to the two actresses, who scrambled back in alarm.

'Don't do that!' Sadie cried out. 'You could kill us all before you get that box open!'

Big Bravo paused. The box was dented and battered but it was still closed. Another blow to Big Bravo's pride!

'You keep your damned mouth shut!' he roared at Sadie. 'Who told you to give an opinion.' He kicked the strongbox and it keeled over with the lid half open . . . and jammed.

Big Bravo strode around like a raging bull goaded in a bullring. His eyes were rimmed with fire and he pointed his Colt every which way, as if he might shoot everyone and everything in sight. Then he walked right up to Sadie Solomon and glowered down at her. 'You a damned witch or something? You put a spell on that box!'

'That's no way to treat a lady,' Jim Sivers said from the shadows. He had positioned himself close to a tree so he could take cover from the big man's wrath. Jim Sivers was no slouch with a gun and Big Bravo knew that.

There was a moment when the air seemed as tense as a bowstring with Jim Sivers standing in shadows and Big Bravo panting with fury.

'OK, boys,' Coyote Ben said. He had stood up and he had his thumbs hooked into his gunbelt. He had a grin on his face but there was a menacing glint to his eyes.

Big Bravo panted for a moment longer and then decided to turn the whole thing into a joke. He reholstered his Colt and stood over the strongbox.

'Just so long as we get this sardine tin open,' he laughed.

The two women sighed and Sadie gave Phoebe a look as if to say, what do we do with these unpredictable *hombres?*

Coyote Ben moved over to the strongbox and gave it a nudge with his foot. The lid fell open as if it had been waiting for the right treatment all the time.

Jim Sivers gave a snigger of laughter. Brokenwheel chuckled. Big Bravo bent over the strongbox and peered inside. 'An Indian blanket!' he said in amazement. 'A damned Indian blanket!'

Coyote Ben crouched down beside the box and jerked the blanket away.

There was a moment of astonished silence. All four of the men were bent over the strongbox peering inside.

'Is this some kind of a joke?' Big Bravo growled.

'Who did this?' Brokenwheel asked.

Coyote Ben capsized the strongbox and a heap of rocks came tumbling out beside the fire.

For what seemed like a year to the two women there was a kind of eerie silence. None of the gang knew what to say or what to do. Sadie felt deeply apprehensive. She knew there was about to be an eruption of some kind, and, which ever way, there had to be a scapegoat — a victim to pick on. She slipped her hand under her bodice and felt the reassuring touch of the derringer. Phoebe had her arms clasped round her knees in a posture of defence and self-protection. What shall we do? her eyes seemed to say.

Big Bravo raised his head and glared around at the others. 'We've been tricked,' he murmured. 'You know that, we've been tricked. Somebody has played us for a bunch of suckers.' His angry eyes rested on Sadie and she looked away, but not too quickly in case he concluded she had something to hide.

At last Big Bravo fixed on Coyote Ben. 'You know what,' he said. 'You were the one who told us they were carrying some kind of rich loot on that stage. As I remember it, you said the floozie you spent the night with in Cimarron told you there would be a strongbox of riches on that stage.'

Coyote Ben shook his head slowly. 'That's the truth,' he admitted. 'Act of revenge of some kind. But what's done is done, after all. No use raving and beating up on ourselves, is there? I guess we should cut our losses and figure out our next move.'

There was another moment of tense silence.

'Tell you what we do,' Jim Sivers said. 'What we do is think about the situation and drink the rest of that booze . . . and maybe entertain these ladies for a while.' He winked in the direction of Sadie and Phoebe.

★ ★ ★

Mav led the Indian pony back to the paddock behind Gladness's place and gave it some feed. Huck whinnied a greeting and the mule raised its head as much as to say, Who the hell are you?

Gladness was on her knees washing down the back steps. She had her working clothes on. The dog Sheridan gave a yap and came to investigate. Josh was working on some tackle in the barn. He came out and stared.

'What's that you brought here, Mr Mav? Why, that's an Indian pony unless I'm a balded-head coot!'

'An Indian pony,' Mav agreed. 'Comanche, unless I'm mistaken.'

Gladness had got up from the step. She came over and rested her hand on Sheridan's neck. 'Why, that's the pony the actor was riding,' she said.

'Right, ma'am,' Mav agreed. 'I'd like with your permission to feed it up good.'

Josh looked wide-eyed at the beast. 'What you aim to do with that pony, Mr Mav?' he asked.

Mav ran his hand over the pony's neck and it quivered slightly. 'What I aim to do is to return it where it came from. To my way of thinking it belongs to an acquaintance of mine.'

Josh looked decidedly uneasy. 'That's a Comanche pony. Someone stole it. Won't they come raiding on the town to get it back?'

Mav was rubbing the stubble on his cheek. 'They won't come raiding, Josh. This pony is a goodwill gesture. Without this pony that actor Joe Basnett would likely be eaten by coyotes and buzzards instead of riding into town with those cruel welts across his back.'

Earlier, Mav had been to the doc's to talk to the actor and Joe Basnett had pleaded with him. 'I saw you when we were about to leave on the stage,' the beat up actor said. 'Thought you looked like a man of action, maybe the only one in this town. Please . . . please,' he said. 'You've got to save those two women!'

Mav was not easily touched. After his mother's death in that cruel fire he had grown a hard protective shell all round him — or thought he had.

'They killed my partner, those vicious beasts!' Joe Basnett cried. 'Why? Why? All for the sake of a box of gold!'

'You rest easy,' Mav reassured him.

But Joe Basnett wasn't finished. He held out something in his hand. 'That Indian knew you were here. He asked me to give you this.'

Mav looked down and saw what Joe Basnett was holding out to him. It was the pendant he had given to Water-that-Runs-in-the-Creek!

* * *

Gladness was quite glum that night over dinner, as though she was secretly grieving again over her lost husband and the little children the Apaches had killed. Josh made signals with his hands from behind her to warn Mav not to rock her boat too much.

At last she raised her eyes and

decided to speak. 'It's just come to me,' she declared. 'Something tells me I have to ask you to leave this house.' She looked down quickly as though in apology.

Mav was chewing a neatly cooked slice of ham and Sheridan was lying out half-asleep on the rug. Mav put his knife aside and nodded slowly. 'If that's what you want,' he said.

Gladness raised her head and looked at him squarely. 'It's not what I want. It's because you're in league with those red men and I don't trust Indians.'

Mav wagged his head from side to side. 'I hear what you're saying, Gladness, and I understand your feelings. Those particular red men you speak of are Comanche and it was Apaches killed your family. Comanche and Apache are rooted enemies, have been for a long time.' He told her about the episode to the east of town when he had saved the Apache boy from Big Bravo and the bunch and how there had been a temporary truce between the Comanche and the Apache.

'That was a brave thing to do,' she agreed. 'But they're still Indians and, after what happened, I can't trust them.'

'There's something I want you to have,' he said. He fumbled about under his chair and brought out a package. He opened it and laid the contents on the table before her. It was a pair of finely beaded moccasins. 'These are the moccasins Rising Cloud, the Comanche chief, gave me,' he said.

Josh was watching him wide-eyed from the corner of the room.

Mav nodded slowly. 'I want you to have these, Gladness, because I aim to leave come sunup anyway. I have to ride out. Got something particular to do. If you can't accept the moccasins, keep them safe for me until I come back, because I will come back. One way or the other I will come back.'

Gladness was looking at him in astonishment. 'These were for you, Mav,' she said.

'For me or for you, it doesn't matter either way,' he replied.

Josh took the hint. He gave a slight bow in Mav's direction and slid sideways out of the room.

Gladness was looking at the moccasins in disbelief. 'I guess what you have in mind. You have some crazy notion you can ride out and save those women and I don't want you to leave for that reason. It may be a brave thing to do but it's foolish and unreal!'

Mav saw she was split in her feelings for him and the Indians.

He considered for a moment. 'There's another reason,' he said. 'I haven't worked it out yet. But it's got something to do with Colonel Dee. He has something against me for what happened back East and yet he's offering me a reward for bringing in those *bandidos*' heads on a plate. Haven't yet figured out his game, but he's playing a deep hand.'

★　★　★

187

Come sunup, Mav was out in the paddock getting Huck ready to leave. He had his saddle-bag loaded with everything necessary.

'Listen up, Huck, we gotta get on the trail. There's work to be done. Could be difficult for both of us. Dangerous too.'

The mule had ambled over as though he didn't mean to be left out and Mav scratched him between the ears. 'Not this time,' he said. 'You're a good boy but you have to stick around and wait till we come back. That's no big deal. Josh is spoiling you fine.'

Josh appeared at the barn door. He looked at Mav with his sad old eyes and nodded mournfully. 'See you're set on leaving us like you said.'

Mav threw the saddle over Huck's back and tightened the cinch. 'The mule's staying. A kind of guarantee we'll be back. Anything bad happens, I want you to take the mule and look after it good like you have been. Could get you back to your family if you treat it right.'

Josh's eyes lit up quickly at the mention of his family. Then he shook his head. 'Long time since I seed them. Probably think the Good Lord has taken me up to the Promised Land in one of those chariots I hear tell about.'

Mav went over to the Indian pony and talked to it quietly. It was inclined to be skittish but it calmed down when it heard the tone of his voice.

Mav mounted Huck and took the pony's rawhide leading rein.

'Tell Miss Letty to keep the cooking pot boiling for when I get back,' he said over his shoulder.

'I'll do that, Mr Mav. I'll sure do that.'

As Mav rode out of the yard, Sheridan emerged from behind the house to give him an encouraging yap. Mav glanced at the house and saw the curtains move slightly. He knew that Gladness was behind them watching him. So he gave her a cut-away salute and rode on.

* * *

Cimarron might be the laziest town in the territory but there were plenty of people about even at that time of the morning. The old man who kept up an eternal vigil outside the Cimarron Grand, for instance. He was there on his rocking-chair. Probably slept there all night, Mav figured. The old geek gave him a flutter of the hand as he passed.

The bank was slumbering with all its dollars and Colonel Dee still lay in bed dreaming of who knew what.

The sun was already up over the sandy desert scrub and it looked as if it would be a hot day. Hot for somebody and a little cold for somebody else, Mav figured.

He followed the trail the Butterfield stage had taken, the trail that led on through scrub and rocky gullies towards Santa Fe, though that was a deal further on.

Somewhere along the trail there was,

according to legend, a waterhole. When he found it, towards midday, he stopped to give the horses a drink and a rest.

'You did good, buddy boy,' he said to Huck. 'Tell this Indian pony he did right well too.' Huck was too busy getting his nose down in the water to take much notice and the Indian pony wasn't interested anyway.

Mav sat down under the spiny trees and took a drink out of his canteen.

When he looked up, he wasn't surprised to see the Indian standing just inside the tree line. Chief Rising Cloud had come, as he had expected.

The chief raised his hand, palm open towards Mav.

'Hi there, Chief.' Mav got up on his feet and the chief came forward to meet him. 'I brought your pony back,' Mav said. 'Thought you might be missing him some.'

They shook hands in the gringo way.

'My brother,' the chief said. 'You have big problems. I come help you.'

Mav nodded. 'That's good,' he said. 'We need all the help we can get. That actor might have died without your help.'

'You get my message?' the chief enquired.

Mav nodded again thoughtfully. 'Glad to get it. Somebody has to round up those killers before they do a deal more harm.' He paused. 'You know where they are right now?'

Chief Rising Cloud twisted his mouth in a grim smile. 'We know. They got those two women prisoner. We help you free them.' He paused and made a chopping motion with his hand. 'We can kill those men. Then your mind is clear. But first you come to our tepee. We talk. Water-that-Runs-in-the-Creek is waiting to greet her brother.'

Mav wanted to ride on and gun down on those killers immediately for the sake of those two women, but he needed Rising Cloud and his Comanche Indians to guide him in. So he rode along with the chief for quite a distance until they came to the Comanche camp.

Water-that-Runs-in-the-Creek was waiting. She was a fine woman and she greeted Mav as his sister . . . or maybe more than a sister.

They sat around the fire and smoked sweet grass and talked. Chief Rising Cloud seemed in no hurry to move on the killers. So Mav settled down to wait. He thought of those two actresses quivering and shaking in fear of their lives, wherever they were.

After they had smoked and eaten their fill Mav expected Rising Cloud to speak. The chief sat thoughtfully for a while, then presently a young brave rode into the camp and conferred with the chief in Comanche.

Rising Cloud stretched out his hand as though smoothing out a blanket. 'Black Dog says the two women are safe but in much danger. The four *bandido* men are drinking and making war about the box they stole from the stage-coach.' He paused to chuckle to himself. 'No frog skins in the box and no gold. Just a bunch of rocks. The big man got riled up about that. Fit to kill.'

Mav nodded slowly and considered the matter. Just a bunch of rocks, he thought. Someone must have known about the intended hold-up.

He knew it was time to move. They had to go in and release the two women. But then he paused and leaned forward intently. 'Listen, Chief. I know Comanche move quietly.'

The chief nodded. 'Those *bandidos* are very bad medicine. It is right we kill them.'

Mav closed one eye in concentration. 'It's not good for you to do the killing,' he said. 'Better for me to do any killing necessary. Better still, we bring them in and hang them high from a tree.'

The chief seemed impressed by the argument. 'We free those women. You kill those bad men. Is that the deal?'

'That's the deal,' Mav said.

★ ★ ★

Coyote Ben, Big Bravo and the others were, in fact, still in the same camp. Sadie Solomon was getting more and more apprehensive and Phoebe had started to cry for her momma. Night was approaching and the bottles were still being passed around. Big Bravo was still raving about the chest full of rocks and Brokenwheel roamed around from time to time, peering through the scrub to the land beyond as though he expected a posse from Cimarron to come riding along the trail.

'You know what,' he said. 'We're like ducks sitting on a pond waiting around here. Be better if we moved on well away from the trail so they can't track us easy. What's your opinion, Ben?'

'You could be right,' Coyote Ben said. He had his stock whip beside him and he was cleaning his shooter as though it was his best buddy.

Big Bravo swung round quickly despite all the booze he had taken in. 'First we have a share-out,' he growled. 'Then we split. Anyone who wants to go to California, that's his choosing. Anyone who wants to go south to Mexico, that's his choice too. Those *señoritas* down there have very welcoming ways, so I hear.'

'What about these two calico queens?' Jim Sivers asked with a grin of relish, as though he was about to eat a big raw steak.

'Either we take them with us or we leave them here,' Brokenwheel suggested.

That caused a ripple of laughter to pass among the men.

'Maybe we should leave them here,' Coyote Ben said. 'It was a damned fool idea to bring them along in the first place.'

'I don't buy that,' Big Bravo said. 'These two queens were part of the deal. We throw them in with the loot and play us a game of poker to share things out.'

'That sounds like a good deal,' Brokenwheel responded. ''Cept I see only two queens here.'

'Winner takes all,' Big Bravo said. 'One who wins can take the spoils and choose the woman he wants. How does that strike you?'

Sadie didn't care for the tone of the conversation and she could see Phoebe was shaking so much she might fall apart. 'Keep yourself calm if you want to live,' she whispered. 'Remember you've still got that little pistol. When the moment comes we could bring two of them down. That way we might survive.'

Big Bravo had produced a deck of cards and he started dealing them out on a blanket. Coyote Ben was sitting back, nursing his shooter.

'You in?' Big Bravo threw at him over his shoulder.

'I don't gamble,' Coyote Ben said.

'What d'you mean, you don't gamble?' Big Bravo said. 'I seen you gamble a hundred times. Didn't we meet in a poker game back there in Kansas?'

Coyote Ben shook his head. 'Lost the taste for it. I'll just take my share of the loot and ride out come sunup.' Sadie saw he had an over-modest look on his face, as if he just become a preacher or something.

'That's no part of the deal,' Big Bravo said.

'What about your share of these two queens?' Brokenwheel asked.

'I don't give a damned about them.' Coyote Ben looked over at the two actresses and gave a leer. 'They got what's coming to them anyway.'

Big Bravo gave a growl of laughter. 'Didn't figure you for a Jesuit,' he jeered.

'Take another drink,' Coyote Ben said. He passed out the bottle and the others each took a swig. That was hard booze and Sadie realized what Coyote Ben was playing at. Big Bravo was still dealing the cards but Brokenwheel and Jim Sivers seemed less and less inclined for the poker game. After an hour Brokenwheel stretched himself out by the fire and was soon snoring like a bull having a fit. Jim Sivers had propped himself against a tree with his hat pulled down over his eyes. He appeared to be asleep.

'Oh hell,' Big Bravo mumbled, then he keeled over and lay on his back.

That left Coyote Ben and the two women staring across the fire at one another.

Coyote Ben waited until everything had quietened to a murmur. Then he got up slowly and moved across to Sadie.

'Listen, and listen good,' he whispered intently. 'You want to live you keep your mouths shut and do what I tell you. You understand?'

Sadie nodded slowly.

'You hear good?' Coyote Ben asked Phoebe.

Phoebe nodded. Though her eyes were wide with terror and she was breathing in gasps, she held herself as quiet as possible.

Coyote Ben had a pistol in one hand and his stock whip hanging from the other. He motioned to the women and they moved out towards the tethered horses.

'Now you each take a horse and we ride out. You hear what I say?'

'Where are you taking us?' Phoebe squeaked.

'That's no never mind to you,' he said. 'You just mount up like I said and we ride out good and slow.'

The two women did as they were told. Coyote Ben had his pistol on them, so they couldn't risk making a noise.

This was Sadie's chance to make a break for it. She reached inside for her derringer just as Coyote Ben swung towards Phoebe. She had the derringer half-drawn when there was a sudden unexpected intervention.

9

Sadie was looking down at Coyote Ben when it happened. Someone had leaped up on the horse behind her. He had his hand over her mouth so she couldn't cry out. Phoebe was halfway to screaming when a second Indian leaped on the back of her horse and she screamed anyway.

Then all hell broke out.

Jim Sivers was on his feet letting loose with his shooter. The Indian behind Sadie jerked and fell.

Big Bravo and Coyote Ben suddenly jumped into life. Big Bravo was grabbing his gun when a Comanche brave sprang at him from behind a tree. The Indian clung round his neck like a monkey, trying to bring him down. Big Bravo swung him round and hurled him right on to the fire. The Indian sprang up with a shriek just as Big

Bravo brought his gun into play and shot him dead.

That shook Brokenwheel into life. He grabbed his Winchester and started pumping off shots every which way. But not for long. The form of another Comanche streaked in and chopped him down with a tomahawk. Brokenwheel fell face down before he knew what had hit him. Jim Sivers fired a shot at the Indian and brought him face down beside the still twitching body of Brokenwheel.

Coyote Ben fired a shot at Phoebe's horse. The horse reared up and capsized slowly like a ship that has hit a rock.

The Indian on the back of Sadie's horse dug his heels into the horse's side. The horse bolted with Sadie and the Indian on its back, leaving Phoebe screaming loud enough to terrify the whole of New Mexico and Arizona!

Now the three killers drew together and formed a triangle, facing outwards. Jim Sivers fired a shot at a fleeing

Comanche. Then he got down on one knee to reload his gun.

Phoebe suddenly recovered enough to seize her chance. She ran off among the scrubby trees towards the trail.

Big Bravo cursed and broke the triangle. He raised his long-barrelled Colt and fired a shot. Phoebe fell and lay like a broken doll without another sound.

Three prairie chickens broke cover and flew off with a gobbling clatter.

'That's for you, bitch!' Big Bravo shouted.

He moved back quickly to reform the triangle.

A slow quietness descended on the scene.

★　★　★

'We got to get out of here,' Coyote said after a moment.

'We sure do,' Jim Sivers said. 'I knew it was the wrong place all the time. Too much cover for those pesky Indians to creep up on us. We got three at least. That's some credit.'

There was a groan from close by the fire. Jim Sivers moved over to investigate. It could have been Brokenwheel, but it was the Indian who had tomahawked him.

Jim Sivers cocked his pistol and shot the dying Indian right through the head. Did him a favour, anyway, he thought as he moved to join the others. 'Pity about Brokenwheel,' he said. 'He could be difficult but he had his good points.'

'Never knew why they called him Brokenwheel,' Big Bravo growled. 'But it turned to be true anyway.' He gave a low cackle of laughter.

Jim Sivers was looking around cautiously. 'Got a lot more than they could chew on,' he said. 'Damned Indians. Thought they didn't come raiding at night.'

'These ones did,' Coyote Ben said ominously. 'Now you boys load up the horses while I stand guard. Then we move out into more open country so they can't sneak up on us any more.'

*　★　*

Mav, mounted on Huck, had been waiting about half a mile away when the shooting broke out. He and Chief Rising Cloud had come to an agreement. The Comanche braves would sneak in and release the two women. Then he would ride in and take the four *bandidos*. It seemed a bad arrangement but it was a matter of honour and he had to consider the chief's dignity. And now it had all gone wrong. He knew that when he saw the forlorn Comanche warrior riding towards him in the semi-darkness. The chief greeted him in the usual way, but Mav saw immediately that everything had been twisted up.

'What happened, my brother?' he asked.

'Three of my young bloods dead,' the chief replied.

No tribe could afford to lose a single brave and the loss of three young men at one time meant big grieving. The chief clearly blamed himself and Mav took much of the blame too. He knew he should have gone in with those Indians and confronted the killers straight away.

Sadie Solomon was in a state of shock. She had kept her head all through the episode and now she broke down. Mav helped her from her horse and made her drink from a canteen.

'They got Phoebe,' she cried. 'Poor kid didn't stand a chance. She ran away screaming and one of those brutes just shot her in the back. What am I going to do?'

Water-that-Runs-in-the-Creek took her gently by the hand and led her away to grieve. These Comanche people have lost three of their young men and this woman can still find it in her heart to comfort Sadie Solomon! That's a true wonder, Mav thought.

He turned to face Rising Cloud

again. Though the chief was grieving, he held himself straight and Mav saw a look of rocklike determination on his riven face.

'You did what you promised,' Mav said. 'Things did not go well for your young men. That is a sad thing. Now I do what I promised.'

Rising Cloud looked at him in surprise. 'First we give respect,' he said. 'We honour those young men. Then we ride after those killers and kill them.'

Mav nodded grimly. 'You grieve and I grieve with you. Then you take Miss Sadie back to Cimarron. There's a time to be sad and a time for revenge. Those killers have to be stopped before they do more damage . . . kill more young men and women.'

The chief bowed his head in acknowledgement.

★   ★   ★

Back in Cimarron Colonel Dee had put on his best tail jacket. He was wearing a fancy cravat, a high collar and a top hat. He was about to call on Gladness again. Josh was polishing up a window and he stood back to admire his work when he glimpsed the colonel riding down Main Street on his best mare.

My! thought Josh, I sure must run round to the back and warn Miss Letitia. Before he got halfway Sheridan came barking and leaping up. So Josh had to bend down and fondle him some.

'Is your mistress in?' the colonel enquired from high up on his horse.

'I'll go see, Colonel Dee, sir,' Josh said, bowing low.

'No need to bother,' the colonel said with a supercilious grin. He swung down from his horse and handed the reins to Josh. 'Just hold my mare a piece while I walk right in.'

Josh stood holding the reins. The horse tossed her head and gave him a look that seemed to match the colonel's with its disdain.

Gladness was out back of the house fixing the down pipe. There had been rain in the night and it had developed a leak.

'What are you doing up there?' the colonel laughed.

'Just fixing the place.' Gladness looked down on him from her ladder. She was dressed in her dungarees and she was holding a hammer. She had a nail in the corner of her mouth.

The colonel gave her a jeering laugh. 'Ever hopeful, I see, Letitia. I guess you'll still be hammering when the place falls in on you. Why don't you just leave it be and I'll send my man round and fix the job?'

'I like to get things done,' she said from her perch.

'Sure you do,' he laughed, 'even if it means flogging a dead horse. Why don't you just come down and talk? I have things to say to you.'

Gladness shrugged and descended. The colonel thought of giving her a hand down but he knew she would shrug him off. So he stood back and waited.

'You want for me to get tea, Miss Letitia?' Josh enquired.

'Leave it,' Gladness said abruptly. She wiped her hands on an old rag and went into the house. The colonel followed her into the parlour and set himself down without ceremony.

'Bit of a wind last night,' he remarked. 'Round about midnight. I guess you heard it too. Thought it might blow the house down like in that story about the three little pigs.'

Gladness had heard the old house creaking like an old galley in a storm. So she knew what he meant . . . knew what he was implying too.

'Had you anything you wanted to say in particular, Colonel?' she asked.

'Well, now,' he said. 'I guess you remember, I made a certain proposal to you about a week gone by. Thought I might drop by to enquire about your thinking on the matter.'

Gladness looked out of the window.

'I haven't had much time for thinking this past week, Colonel. I've been too busy.'

Colonel Dee nodded reflectively. 'These are lean times, Letitia. I guess you noticed that?'

'Times are lean,' Gladness admitted, 'but we manage to keep our heads above water, don't we?' She spoke with a hint of irony in her voice since Colonel Dee owned most of the town.

'See your visitor Mr Jesse Bolder pulled out. And you have no other paying guest around the house. Can't make things any easier.'

She gave the colonel a level look. 'He didn't pull out. He just rode out to return the Indian pony to its master.'

'That's no big deal,' the colonel agreed, 'but I think he had other intentions too. And I guess you know that.'

'What would they be?' she asked defiantly.

'I did hear,' he said, 'he intended to track down on those bank robbers and

211

killers and either shoot them dead or bring them back alive . . . a somewhat impossible task, I think you'll agree?'

Gladness shuddered deep in her soul.

'Of course, that Jesse Bolder, or Maverick as he chooses to call himself, could have another idea too . . . ' the colonel said.

'And what might that be, Colonel?'

Colonel Dee looked thoughtful. 'Could be he intends to pick up the chest of gold they stole from the coach and ride on with it into the sunset.'

Gladness took in a breath and said nothing for a moment. Could it be so? she wondered.

' 'Cept that, if he does that, he's in for one big disappointment,' the colonel said.

Gladness didn't say: why should that be? as he had hoped.

'You know why that is, Letitia?' he asked.

Gladness gave an almost imperceptible shake of her head.

'That is because there's no gold or

dollars or any other riches in that chest,' the colonel told her. 'You know why?'

Again Gladness shook her head. She could scarcely bring herself to speak.

The colonel took up his hat and gave a low growl of humourless laughter. 'That's because there is nothing valuable in that chest. You see, I had it packed with rocks. Don't you think that's real smart?'

Gladness paused for a moment. Then she reached out, took the colonel's top hat and thrust it against his chest. 'I think you'd better take that and leave!' she said.

Colonel Dee was laughing as he went to the door. If you can't succeed in love, be cruel: that was his policy.

After he had left she sat for a moment in deep thought. Then she got up slowly and went to the window. The colonel was riding leisurely back towards the bank.

'All those people killed,' she said to herself. 'All those men and women slain for a chest full of rocks.'

She was about to sit down at the table when Josh gave his usual knock and came in.

'Miss Letitia,' he said in an uncertain tone. 'You have another visitor.'

'Who's that?' she said.

Before Josh could reply, a tall woman came in boldly, waving him aside. It was Brassy Baby.

Gladness rose in astonishment. She knew Brassy Baby well and she knew her reputation. But this was no usual Brassy Baby. She had no fancy outfit and no garish makeup on. This was a Brassy Baby dressed for the road and ready to ride.

'Surprised to see me, Mrs Bean?' she said. 'Tell you the truth, I'm surprised myself.'

'Why don't you sit down?' Gladness said. 'I'll have Josh bring tea.'

Josh gave a start of surprise. His jaw had fallen somewhat and his eyes were popping.

'Don't bother with tea,' Brassy Baby

said. 'I'm not here for tea.' She sat down on the chair the colonel had vacated. 'I'm here because I have an idea that might interest you.'

'What's that?' Gladness asked suspiciously.

Brassy Baby spread her hands on the table as though she was laying out her plan. 'I guess I've been too long in that Cimarron Grand Hotel and it's time to move on. So I'm clearing out.' She shifted to a more comfortable position on the chair. 'A person can spend too much of her life hanging around getting a bad reputation for herself. I done a lot of bad things, Mrs Bean, and that's the truth, but I've been listening to that actor's story and I know your guest who calls himself Maverick has gone looking for those killers. I plan on helping him best way I can even if it's the only good thing I ever did.'

Gladness looked at her wide-eyed for a moment, then sat down opposite her. Was this woman crazy or something?

'But you can't ride out there in the

wilderness alone. Where would you go? What could you do?'

Brassy Baby nodded and gave her a broad grin. 'I guess you think I'm half-crazy. But I'm serious on this.' She reached under her jacket and brought out a Smith & Wesson thirty-two. 'You see this?' she said. 'Well, it ain't just a toy. I can use it. I've been practising good. I was a sharpshooter in a fair back East one time. I put a can on the fence and pretended it was that brute Big Bravo and it worked. I can hit that can three times out of three when I picture his big ugly abusive mug.' She laid the Smith & Wesson on the table.

Gladness stared at it for a full ten seconds. 'I understand your sentiments and I wonder what you expect me to do?'

Brassy Baby picked up the revolver and spun it. 'I guess I'm offering you the chance to come with me,' she said.

She looked up into Gladness's eyes and held them for a moment. 'None of my business,' she said, 'but I figure you and me have something in common.'

Gladness was too wise to contradict her. 'You may be right. I don't know a lot about you,' she said.

'I know a deal about you,' Brassy Baby said. 'I heard about your husband and those two baby girls of yours, and I know how Colonel Dee is tormenting you. And I know another thing too . . . ' She paused and looked closely into Gladness's eyes. 'I know you're worried about that man who has been lodging here, calls himself Maverick.'

'You know all these things,' Gladness said. 'But you haven't said what you want . . . what you intend.'

Brassy Baby got up from the table deliberately. 'I'm offering you the chance to ride with me. We take enough food for three or four days. We go out looking for Maverick. Then we help him bring in those killers, so we can hang them high from the gallows tree.'

This woman is plumb crazy, Gladness thought.

Come sunup Big Bravo, Coyote Ben, and Jim Sivers were jogging along on the flat country with rocky outcrops on their left. Not much chance for anyone to creep up through the chaparral and gun down on them there. But Jim Sivers was uneasy. He had a creepy feeling around his neck that they were being tracked and watched. He was riding slightly behind the other two, and from time to time he paused to glance round and look for movements. Those Indians had rare tracking skills and he knew they would be out for revenge. He also had a feeling in his bones that the man called Maverick might be involved. Like Big Bravo he had had a creepy notion about that *hombre* since the incident with the Apache Indian.

Coyote Ben reined in suddenly and looked back along the trail. 'You know what,' he said. 'That idea about staying out here on the flat lands was not so hot after all.'

'You don't think so?' Big Bravo said. 'Why should that be?'

'Why that should be,' Coyote Ben said, 'is those Comanche Indians prefer the open range. Suits their tactics better. They like to ride in on a person and shoot him down before he can get himself together.'

'That was in the old days,' Big Bravo said, 'when a man had to stop to reload after the first shooting. That's when you were liable to get skewered by those long lances they carried.'

Jim Sivers was caught both ways. He couldn't make up his mind whether they should head for the crags or ride on through the flat country.

'We make good progress we reach Little Springs before sundown,' Big Bravo said. 'We can rest up there for a piece before we ride on to Santa Fe.'

The thought of Santa Fe and a time of rest appealed to Jim Sivers, but he fumbled in his saddle-bag and produced a small telescope. He scanned the country behind them to left and right and saw what he feared — a faint cloud of dust rising from behind a stand of cactus.

'We got to make up our minds,' he said, 'Cos we're being tailed.'

'Let me have that!' Big Bravo grabbed the telescope and scanned the desert. 'Just a little bit of dust,' he said. 'Could be an animal or anything.'

'That little bit of dust means a rider, maybe more than one,' Jim Sivers said. 'That could be there's someone on our tail.'

Coyote Ben took his turn with the telescope. 'By my reckoning that's just one rider,' he said. 'And that makes our decision for us. We ride up among those rocks and bide our time. That rider either goes on along the trail or he tries to come up on us among the rocks like a damned fool. We just shoot him down and then ride on to Little Springs.'

'That sounds right,' Big Bravo said. ''Cept there might be more than one rider. Those Comanches might be circling round.'

'Like you mentioned,' Coyote Ben said, 'Comanches don't have the taste for fighting among the rocks. It ain't their style.'

'How do you figure they're Comanches anyway.' Jim Sivers said. 'Could have been some other tribe. Could have been Apaches.'

'I know Comanches,' Coyote Ben said. 'Those Indians who sneaked in on our camp were definitely Comanches.'

He turned his mount towards the crags and the other two followed through the low chaparral.

★　★　★

Brassy Baby and Gladness rode out of Cimarron together. Gladness had had more than second thoughts about riding with Brassy Baby but had decided in favour of it. It was more of a hunch than a rational decision. Something about Brassy Baby had given her a kind of hope and courage.

Josh was astonished but he accepted

the situation. He was well able to look after the house and everything while Letitia was away, but he was puzzled: why should Letitia make such a fool of herself? Was it something to do with Colonel Dee's visit? Josh always watched and listened but he didn't pick up on everything. So he was bewildered.

Colonel Dee was in the bank when they passed, shouting and raving at his chief clerk. He had to vent his frustration on someone! He turned suddenly and stared open mouthed. Two women — two totally different women — were riding by on their horses. They were dressed somewhat like men and it looked like they were armed!

Gladness and Brassy Baby rode out of town at a gentle jog. Both looked straight ahead as though intent on some strange unexplained venture, but explanation came soon enough. When they were several miles out of town they saw a bunch of riders coming towards them slowly.

'That's Indians!' Brassy Baby exclaimed.

'They're coming right on to us. What do we do?' It seemed some of her courage had already started to ebb away.

Gladness stiffened her back. 'We ride straight on to meet them,' she said. 'We show no fear. That's what we do.'

'They got a woman with them,' Brassy Baby said in surprise. 'They've got a prisoner. Looks like . . . why, that's Sadie Solomon, one of those actresses those killers took from the stage.'

Gladness counted six Indians and saw that Sadie Solomon was riding free. 'I don't think she's a prisoner,' she said. Sadie Solomon looked somewhat dishevelled and her clothes were torn and dirty after her time as a prisoner of the killers, but when she saw the two women riding towards her, she cried out and waved. Was it a cry of relief or a warning, Gladness wondered.

The group of Comanche drew to a halt with their feathers fluttering. A young brave rode forward to meet Gladness and Brassy Baby. He held up his hand, palm towards them and said something in Comanche.

'What is he saying,' Brassy Baby asked.

Gladness didn't understand Comanche and she had started to shake. She had some understanding of the difference between Comanche and Apache but to her Indians were Indians and it was Indians who had slaughtered her husband and her two children.

She was halfway to raising her pistol when Sadie Solomon rode forward. 'These men saved me!' she cried. 'Those killers shot Phoebe but these men saved me and three of them died!'

★　★　★

Mav was riding alone. That was part of his bargain with Rising Cloud. He could see the three killers riding ahead and he knew he was on a damned fool errand, but something irrational drove him on.

'I see those killers way ahead,' he said to Huck. 'Now it's up to me and you.

After all those killings somebody has to act and that's what we must do.'

He rose in his stirrups so that he could see his quarry more clearly: three riders, one of them stopping to look back.

'Those ornery killers think they can ride on to Little Springs,' he said to Huck. 'But I think they're having second thoughts about that.'

He narrowed his eyes and saw the killers suddenly veer off to the left through the chaparral. They're heading for the rocks up there, to that gully, he thought. That way they can look on me and shoot me down. That's what they think, anyway.

He knew that he was behaving like a reckless fool. One man against three and those three hunkered down among the rocks in good sniping positions. What does a man do in those circumstances?

Yet already he had a plan forming in his head. He wouldn't go back or wait for those Comanches to come to his aid. They might take a week over their grieving. So he had to go ahead and act on his own.

He could see the place where the killers had ridden up along a deep gully to wait for him. So he rode in close to the rocks, where he was hidden from view. Maybe he could find a way up among the rocks so he could get level with them or even above them.

He found a shady place and a small pool and dismounted.

'Now you wait along here,' he said to Huck. 'You wait and I climb up. You hear me?'

Huck's ears twitched and he concentrated on getting his wind.

Mav took his Winchester carbine and checked it. He checked his Colt. Then he started to climb.

Mav was no mountaineer but he knew what he wanted. Yet as he heaved himself up he also knew his task was near impossible. It's easy to lose your sense of direction when you're climbing up among the boulders, snaking this way and that way to avoid loose rocks.

Tough and sharp climbing too. A man has to pause for a while and take in big gulps of breath and it's then he realizes he's a damned fool trying to do this goddamned foolish thing.

He might lose direction or even be tempted to back off and think of a better strategy.

But something happened to guide him. He suddenly heard a voice calling off to his right: 'Is that you, Scarecrow?' the voice called out, slightly above him. 'You there, Scarecrow?' it said. 'Did you get your pants on yet?' The voice followed up with a loud guffaw that was suddenly cut short.

★ ★ ★

The voice was the voice of Jim Sivers. He was perched up on a high point overlooking the plain below. He felt invincible and in the mood to mock.

'Shut your mouth!' Coyote Ben growled. 'You want to bring the whole neighbourhood in?'

Big Bravo sniggered. What neighbour-hood? he thought as he looked down over the plain. Nothing but gophers and prairie chickens. That's no neighbour-hood! He was settling himself into a relatively comfortable position from where he could command the route up and shoot down anyone approaching.

Coyote Ben was lying out on a flat rock under an overhang somewhat higher up. He had his shooter beside him and his whip curled like a snake ready to strike.

The horses were moving restively in a shady position further down.

'You know what?' Jim Sivers said. 'That crazy fool can't come up here without getting himself shot. And we can't go down neither. Could be here till doomsday. Did you think of that, Big Bravo?'

'I thought of it,' Big Bravo agreed. 'We just have to bide our time. Wait for that fool to make the first move.'

'Keep your voices down,' Coyote Ben advised.

10

'What are you doing here?' Sadie Solomon asked.

Brassy Baby and Gladness exchanged cautious glances.

'What we're doing is looking for those killers,' Brassy Baby said.

'What d'you aim to do when you find them?' Sadie said. 'They already killed Phoebe and three Indians. Those aren't men, they're wild beasts. They care for no man and no woman.'

Gladness looked puzzled. She was beginning to realize that their mission was insane. 'Now we got Sadie maybe we should escort her back to Cimarron. Make sure she's safe.' she said.

The Comanche braves were giving them searching looks. Then one of them, a youth of no more than seventeen, urged his mount forward. 'You go back to Cimarron,' he said in

English. 'That is best thing. You go back. We join our brothers. Ride on, help your brother.'

'Where's Mav?' Gladness said.

Sadie gave an account of what had happened and the fact that Mav had ridden out alone in pursuit of the killers.

'But that's a crazy thing to do!' Gladness said.

Sadie explained that the Comanches had to grieve for the three dead Indians and that Mav had decided not to wait but to follow the trail while it was still fresh.

'He's an impulsive crazy fool!' Brassy Baby declared.

'What can we do?' Gladness asked desperately.

'You know where those killers are headed?' Brassy Baby asked the Indian.

The Indian nodded. 'We help you,' he said. 'We go after those men who killed our brothers and we kill them.'

Only if you get there before they kill Mav, Gladness thought.

Jim Sivers was getting restless again. He was tempted to raise his head to see if he could spot Mav riding in on his horse. Come closer, Scarecrow, he thought. Just come within range and I shall have the pleasure of lifting you out of your saddle and crashing you down like a dead bird on the sand.

Yet everything below had become eerily quiet, except for a few buzzards circling in high anticipation of blood. You won't be disappointed, Jim Sivers thought. We already gave you two good meals and another one is on its way. He chuckled and raised his head above his rocky perch.

'Keep your head down, you crazy coot!' Big Bravo growled.

That gave Mav the clue he was waiting for. He had now climbed a considerable way up and figured he might be almost on a level with the killers — possibly even slightly above them. He had had to take snaking action to avoid starting a minor landslide and one or two rocks had bounced down in the direction of the plain below. When that happened he froze and listened before moving on cautiously. He could hear the occasional voice, mostly Jim Sivers's high-pitched carolling tone; that was when he listened, checked his position, then moved on.

He raised his head cautiously above a rock and looked out. Nothing. Not a sign.

Then Jim Sivers spoke again. 'You think he got cold feet?' he asked.

'Cold feet, my arse!' Big Bravo growled back. It was clear he was getting really irritated about Jim Sivers who couldn't keep his damned mouth shut.

Mav could hear from their voices that they were quite close, maybe a stone's throw away. He raised his head cautiously above the rock and glimpsed Jim Sivers raising himself and looking out to watch the desert below. Just his head and his upper torso and the barrel of his Winchester.

I could take him now, Mav figured. I could take him out before he knew what hit him. That might be the best way. But Mav was no killer and he always hesitated before squeezing the trigger.

'Tell you something,' Jim Sivers complained. 'I guess we figured it wrong. That was just a deer or something making us look a bunch of fools. I think I'll pull out now and take my chance.'

Big Bravo chuckled maliciously. 'Didn't figure you for such a damned fool!' he growled. 'You pull out now you pull out alone. And you don't get any of that loot Ben's got stashed away in his saddle-bag from the bank job.'

'I'll take a chance on that,' Jim Sivers chirped. His head came up above the rock high enough for Mav to take a shot, then it disappeared abruptly. Mav heard him slithering away among the scree. Then there was a loud shot. Must have come from Big Bravo, Mav figured.

He couldn't see what happened next, but a few minutes later he caught the sound of horse's hoofs and Big Bravo cursing. So Sivers got himself free, he thought. That leaves two.

'Damned fool!' Big Bravo swore. 'Got clean away. Might have winged him but I think I missed.'

'Pity you missed!' Mav heard Coyote Ben say. 'He must have taken the horses and that means he got my saddlebag!'

'I can still bring him down!' Big Bravo said. He hauled his considerable weight up from behind the rocks and levelled his Winchester. 'I got a bead on him,' he said. 'Get this!' he shouted as he pumped off several shots at the fleeing Sivers.

Mav's scruples had suddenly cleared. He pushed his Winchester forward and fired a single shot. He saw Big Bravo rear back suddenly with the impact of the bullet. But he wasn't dead! Big Bravo pulled himself round with a curse and looked right up at Mav. 'Why you yellow-bellied saddle tramp!' he roared. 'So you want shooting, do you?'

He fired two shots in quick succession. The second shot caught Mav square in the left arm. Thrust him back like a mailed fist. His Winchester went slithering and bouncing down among the rocks and he lost his grip. Before he could stop himself, he was sliding down among the scree with rocks cascading and bouncing all round him.

Then he blacked out!

When he came round he didn't know how long he had been out. Could have been an hour, could have been a minute. In fact, it was only a matter of seconds. He shook himself conscious and felt the warmth of his own blood seeping from his left arm which hung limp and useless — useless but for the roaring pain!

He shook his head again and tried to take stock of his position. By chance or providence he had come to rest on a narrow ledge. An inch or two over and he would have fallen, probably to his death. He couldn't crawl back and he couldn't go down without falling and sliding some twenty feet below. He could only edge forward along the ledge which curled on forward.

He lay for a moment, trying to get his wind. I lie here too long I'll pass out from loss of blood, he thought. What a damned stupid way to die!

He pushed himself forward until he was lying under an overhang. Then he heard a voice from above.

'Did he get you, Scarecrow?' Coyote Ben said from somewhere above but closer than he would have expected.

He held his breath for a moment and clenched his teeth to fight off the pain in his arm. He summoned his strength and eased slowly forward. There was only one way. The ledge widened out and ran into a slope. That was where they had climbed up, he figured. Big Bravo was slightly higher up on a shelf and Coyote Ben must be no more than five feet above the overhang.

'You down there, Scarecrow?' Coyote Ben called out. 'I hear you breathing. I guess Big Bravo winged you. Why don't you crawl out and let me finish you off?'

Mav lay gasping. He wasn't going to speak and give his position away. He knew if he lay there long enough he would pass out again. If he didn't get some kind of tourniquet on his arm he was likely to bleed to death anyway!

As he lay trying to figure out what to do, he heard a hiss like the hiss of a giant snake and then a sharp crack! Coyote Ben was trying to lash him with that damned stock whip from above, and Ben was no amateur.

'Come on out of there, little man!' Coyote hooted. 'Don't cower like a yellow bellied lizard! Come out and show yourself! Lift your head so I can strike it off! This little tool of mine can do that. It can send your head bouncing off down the crags, gaping and dead like in the French Revolution!'

The whip came down over and over again like a tongue of flame striking the rock above Mav's head. Crack! whack! Crack again! And the last crack found its mark. It whipped right across Mav's face and opened a big bloody welt. Mav let out an involuntary cry.

That was when Coyote Ben smelt blood and went mad. 'Come out of there, you creepy rat!' he shouted. He was on his knees, peering over the edge of his perch, trying to get a fix on Mav so he could lash him to death. The whip came in again and again, lashing Mav's shoulder and the side of his head. Each time he drew back involuntarily to avoid the next lash. The pain in his head crashed out the searing pain in his arm and he knew he couldn't last a moment longer.

That was when Coyote made his big mistake. He stood up and caught his breath and raised the whip above his head to strike down as hard as he could.

The next blow struck the rock so close it could have ripped out Mav's eye. Then there was a momentary pause before the next strike. Mav sensed that Coyote Ben had half winded himself with the exertion. In an instant Mav's head cleared as if a searchlight had been switched on suddenly.

As the whip came down again his right hand reached out instinctively and he gripped the leather thong. Coyote Ben went to tug it out of his grasp, but Mav held on and pulled. He wanted to wrench that damned whip out of the man's hand, but Coyote Ben held on half a second too long! He gave a yell enough to chill the blood of any wild beast in the valley below. Mav saw him pitching forward. For an instant he saw the terror in Coyote Ben's eyes. He felt the whip go slack and lose its power and saw the man's shooter flying free where it had been thrown from its holster.

Then came the crunch of the body as it crashed head first against the slope. Coyote Ben was lying spread-eagled on the rocks with blood seeping from his head into the sand. There was no way he could rise again, Day of Judgment or no Day of Judgment!

Mav fell forward and hugged the rock close. He was shaking and fit to weep, but he was still conscious.

But it wasn't over yet. He heard a sliding among the scree. He looked up and saw Big Bravo slithering down towards him. In his right hand he had that damned long-barrelled Colt revolver.

* * *

Big Bravo came roaring on like a goaded bull. He was covered in his own blood, as though he had been stabbed in a dozen places, but his eyes were bolting out of his head and he was raving. No words came from his lips, but he roared on with the force of an express train driven by a mad cabman! If he didn't stop he would slide right past Mav and go right on into the flatlands below.

But he did stop. He ground his boots

into the rocky slope and came to a halt. He swayed for a second, caught his breath and raised that wicked long-barrelled Colt. He steadied it to take a shot at Mav. Why you, no-good ornery bastard, his lips seemed to shape.

He brought that gun down and steadied it with both hands to take his shot. That gave Mav the chance he needed. It was too late to reach for his own shooter but Coyote Ben's weapon lay where it had fallen, just within reach. His breath was racing but he found enough strength to grab it, cock it and, if it still worked, to take a shot at the descending monster.

Both weapons blasted off almost at the same instant. The two shots blended like the crack of doomsday. Big Bravo staggered and fell over sideways with an expression of outrage and astonishment in his eyes.

Mav lay with his face in the dust.

Big Bravo lay for an instant panting like a wounded buffalo. Then he raised himself on one elbow and squinted down the barrel for a second shot. But the shot never came. Big Bravo keeled over behind a boulder with his eyes staring sightlessly at the clear blue sky.

★ ★ ★

Gladness and Brassy Baby were riding on the flatland when they heard the shooting. Chief Rising Cloud was with them. He had joined the band of Comanches shortly after they met with the Comanche braves. Water-that-Runs-in-the-Creek was there too.

Gladness was still apprehensive about Indians but she had settled down a deal since the braves seemed so friendly and well-disposed towards Mav, the man they called their brother.

Chief Rising Cloud looked wary and concerned. Maybe he was having second thoughts about leaving Mav to go after those killers on his own. He knew Mav was brave but he hadn't realized how foolhardy he was.

Suddenly the chief raised his hand

242

and stopped dead. They could see the reason why. A bunch of horses was coming towards them. They counted four saddle horses, but there was only one rider. He was riding fast as though he had a swarm of angry hornets on his tail. He was riding so fast, he hadn't seen the Comanches and the women riding towards him. When he did see them, he turned the whole bunch of horses as fast as maybe and attempted to ride off in another direction.

The chief said nothing, but he gave a wave of his hand. The Indians and the women started off in hard pursuit. Those Comanche mustangs were noted for their endurance and the rider ahead stood little chance of outpacing them. He turned under a wide-spreading tree and raised his Winchester.

The chief held up his arm again and brought the Indians and the women to a halt. He scrutinized the man under the tree and his eyes narrowed. 'That is one who killed my sons,' he said.

Gladness shivered in her soul. What's

happened to Mav? she wondered.

Then Brassy Baby spoke up. 'You drop that gun down and get right off that horse and raise your hands above your head,' she ordered.

Jim Sivers had a practical turn of mind. He had already saved his skin once on that day and he knew he had to save it again. But he saw all those Comanche Indians and two women, one of whom he recognized as Brassy Baby despite her unaccustomed attire, and he couldn't figure quite what to do.

But Jim Sivers was as creepy and crafty as a rattler and his mind worked like lightning. 'It's OK,' he shouted. 'I got away! I brought the horses. There's no chance Big Bravo and Coyote Ben can ride out since I got their horses.'

'Like hell you got their horses, you sidewinder!' Brassy Baby cried out. 'We heard shooting!'

'You heard shooting. That's because that *hombre* calls himself Maverick got them pinned down up there in the gully. I'll show you the way.'

Brassy Baby shook her head. 'You were in on that bank job,' she said. 'There were five raiders and you were one of them.'

Jim Sivers's brain was still working overtime. 'I was there,' he said, 'but I didn't do no killing. And I got the loot.' He held up Coyote Ben's saddle-bag and shook it. 'I was bringing it back to hand it in. The only reason I was in on that bank job was Coyote Ben had a gun on me. I didn't want to be in on that job but Coyote Ben and Big Bravo made me. Nothing I could do about it. Look . . . ' He shook the bag of loot again. 'I got the money, didn't I? That proves it. And I got a flesh wound in my arm where Big Bravo winged me. Look.' He held up his right arm and there was the stain of blood on his shoulder. 'I was going to shoot it out with Big Bravo but I saw my chance and pulled out! Thought I could get help.'

Gladness saw the desperate look in his eyes and knew he was lying, but she was more intent on getting to Mav as fast as they could. 'You know where Mav is?' she asked.

'Sure do,' Jim Sivers piped up hopefully. 'He's up there. He got those killers pinned down. That's how I made my break.'

One of the young braves was conferring with the chief. Chief Rising Cloud nodded and spoke up. 'You killed my sons,' he said. 'You shot Little Horse right through the head as he lay on the ground.'

Jim Sivers opened his mouth in feigned astonishment. 'I didn't kill no man!' he protested. 'I was acting in self-defence. I wouldn't kill a grasshopper.'

The Indians didn't exactly laugh at that, but Chief Rising Cloud gave a grim nod. 'You put down that shooter you're holding and give yourself up!'

Give myself up to a bunch of wild Indians! Jim Sivers thought. His mind was switching every which way, trying to figure his chances. Which would he prefer, being ripped apart by wild Comanche Indians or swinging from the gallows tree? Could he still talk his way through this and, maybe, even claim a reward for turning in Coyote Ben and Big Bravo.

'They're up there!' he said. 'I'll lead you right to them. They won't stand a chance in hell against you.'

Brassy Bay and Gladness had had enough. Brassy Baby urged her mount forward and levelled her Smith & Wesson. 'Throw that gun away!' she shouted. 'Just drop it on the sand or I'll kill you dead!'

Jim Sivers switched his attention to Brassy Baby and saw in an instant that she meant what she said. Maybe he remembered the time back in the Cimarron Grand Hotel when she had been painted up like a fancy doll. Maybe he figured she couldn't use that shooter.

Whatever he figured, he swung that Winchester right round at her and tried to fire it. But Jim Sivers never got to fire that Winchester. Instead, he was lifted from the saddle. He pitched right back over the horse's rump where he sprawled with his arms flung wide and his mouth open in sheer astonishment.

The horses spooked and reared, but the Comanche braves rode in immediately to steady them down.

The body of Jim Sivers slid back over the horse's rump and lay face up on the sand.

* ★ ★

Brassy Baby stared at the smoking barrel of her Smith & Wesson in dumb astonishment for a moment. Then she looked at Gladness and gasped. 'I killed a man! You know that? I killed a man.'

Gladness reached out to comfort her. 'He would have killed you,' she said.

She was thinking about the gully where the shots had come from. The Comanche were thinking about it too. The chief gave his orders and they moved on with three of the braves scouting ahead. Just a mile or so further on they came upon Mav's horse, Huckleberry, grazing by the pool.

That was not the best omen, Gladness thought. A shiver of apprehension quivered in her body and now Brassy Baby reached out to comfort her.

When they came to the gully an eerie silence reigned. Nobody spoke and the Indians rode ahead.

Chief Rising Cloud was forging ahead and he threw up his arm for the braves to stop. Then he rode on alone up the rocky trail. He could read where the scree had been displaced. Almost immediately he saw two bodies, one of them face down with its head bashed in and the other tilted to one side staring up at the sky in glazed astonishment. The first was Coyote Ben and the other was Big Bravo.

Just to the left a little higher he heard a faint groan. Turning, he saw Mav lying on his side, his left arm saturated with blood.

Gladness and Brassy Baby had pushed on close behind the chief. Both dismounted almost simultaneously and clambered up to the ledge where Mav lay. Close behind them came Water-that-Runs-in-the-Creek.

All three women bent over Mav and tried to comfort him. Gladness and Brassy Baby were crying and Brassy Baby dashed back her tears with the back of her hand.

Water-that-Runs-in-the-Creek made low keening noises in her throat.

Mav's eyes were dazed as if he was only half in this world. Gladness cradled his head and raised it gently, and he managed a smile. His lips shaped a question: 'Did we get them?'

'We got them,' Gladness soothed. 'We got them all.' Mav tried to say, 'That's good . . . ' but his lips quivered and he passed out.

11

When the cavalcade rode in to Cimarron, Colonel Dee was striding up and down inside the bank giving his bald-headed manager the strength of his own opinions on bank security. The manager was shaking at the knees and the teller was trying to hide himself behind the screen.

The main door swung open and the old geek called Skinny Billy came scooting in. ' 'Scuse the interruption!' he shouted in his high squeaky tone. 'Had to come in and tell you, Colonel Dee, sir. Seems we're bein' attacked by Injuns, Comanche by the looks of them.'

The colonel had just raised his finger to deliver another metaphorical blow to his manager when he stopped and swung round.

'What d'you mean, you braying jackass!' he cried.

'Don't believe me, come look fer yerself!' old Skinny Billy crowed. 'They're riding right up Main Street this very moment.'

Colonel Dee left the gawping manager and strode to the window.

He saw the procession which was impressive for a place like Cimarron. A whole bunch of Indians — Comanche as Skinny Billy had said — riding boldly, you could say proudly, down the middle of Main Street. It was the first time Indians had ridden into Cimarron apart from the few that dropped in occasionally on the trading mission about half a mile out of town. So, quite apart from what followed, this was a unique event.

The procession was led by Chief Rising Cloud and Water-that-Runs-in-the-Creek who rode with great dignity as if they were escorting some kind of royal personage, which is what they were doing in their own estimation.

Behind the chief and Water-that-Runs-in-the-Creek came Mav's horse

Huckleberry with Maverick himself propped up in the saddle with his head bloody and his left arm in a sling. The colonel shivered involuntarily and Skinny Billy said: 'My, that sure is something!'

After Mav came three more horses, with bodies lying draped across their backs. These were the earthly remains of the three killers.

After them rode three women, Gladness and Brassy Baby and Sadie Solomons who rode as proudly as the Queen of Sheba.

The procession passed on until it arrived at the Cimarron Grand Hotel. There Chief Rising Cloud raised his hand and the whole troop came to a halt. Three of the Comanche braves stepped down from their mustangs. They dragged the bodies of the killers from their horses and dumped them like sacks of grain on to the dust of Main Street. The Indian dragging Big Bravo off his horse needed a little help to heave him into position, but, after a moment, the three killers were lying side by side face up in a grotesque row.

The chief looked down on the corpses with an expression of contemptuous dignity. Then he raised his arm and gave a signal. The Comanches turned slowly and rode out of town.

★　★　★

That left Gladness, Brassy Baby, Sadie Solomons . . . and Mav. Word had spread like a prairie fire through the community and men and women and children had flocked down to the Grand Cimarron to witness the grim procedures. Some of the children had gathered round the corpses to gawp at their sightless faces.

'Are those men really dead?' one girl marvelled.

'Come away,' the schoolmistress said. 'It's a disgrace leaving those dead people lying abandoned on the street like that.'

The crowd murmured its agreement

but nobody moved to drag the dead men away until the funeral director arrived with his assistant. He had had a prosperous time with the burying of the two actors and the stage driver and the man riding shotgun on the Butterfield stage.

Mav was still sitting astride Huckleberry and he looked ready to drop.

Josh had watched the whole thing. He had been one of the first to see the procession and he had started to wail, fearing the worst. Now he ran forward to help his mistress down from her mount.

'Now, Miss Letitia, we be all here to offer our support,' he said.

The whole crowd gave a murmur of agreement. 'At least you came home in one piece,' old Skinny Billy said.

'That's right,' someone else agreed.

'Clear the way!' Colonel Dee shouted. 'Get this man down from his horse and take care not to cause him more pain.'

The people started to cheer as Mav was helped down from Huckleberry.

* * *

When they buried the actors, Josh had suddenly started to quote: ''I will lift up mine eyes to the hills, from whence cometh my help'.' Then, right there, with all those people present, he began to sing in a good, rich voice. Some thought this was strange. Some folk thought that a black man who had once been a slave had no right to speak out so, and singing was thought to be somewhat outrageous. Maybe he was slightly touched by the sun or had been hitting the booze too hard, but he just carried on singing and presently a lot of folk joined in and the whole burial place vibrated with that sad, hopeful psalm.

'That black man may be a coon,' someone said disrespectfully, 'but he sure has a fine singing voice.' Even Colonel Dee had to agree.

Though Mav was still weak from loss of blood he had had a couple of days to rest up and he insisted on being there too. Brassy Baby was standing head-bowed beside Gladness, holding her arm in support. The two women had grown as close as sisters. Everyone in town noticed that, some with disapproval and some with wonder — a witch teaming up with a calico queen. Truth was that Brassy Baby no longer looked like a calico queen. She looked more like the Queen of Sheba every day.

Colonel Dee was standing a little behind the main party. He had on his best frock coat and he held his top hat close to his chest. His moustache had been oiled up neat and he looked, to Brassy Baby's eyes, like a smart dummy dressed up for the window of a big store. Gladness had seen it too, but she had also noticed something else. Colonel Dee was somewhat paler than usual and he had a strange look in his eyes. It wasn't sadness exactly and it wasn't defeat either. Chastened: maybe that was the word.

After the funeral Gladness held a little gathering in her shaky old house.

Though it was a sad occasion some people became a little raucous. There was even a certain amount of laughter, subdued and relieved. It's so good to be a survivor when someone else has died specially when life hangs by such a thin thread. Josh had laid out quite a spread. He had taken good care of Huckleberry and the mule without a name. He considered it as a privilege and an honour to Mav for whom he had formed considerable respect.

★   ★   ★

A week later, still with his arm in a sling, Mav stepped over to the colonel's office. He had a gunny sack in his hand and he swung it on to the colonel's desk, where he let it lie.

'What's this?' the colonel asked although he knew already. Dollar bills and gold coins were spilling out over the desk.

'That's the loot those killers stole when they robbed the bank and killed the sheriff,' Mav said laconically. 'Thought you might like it back but I couldn't come before on account I was slightly indisposed.' Mav was still pale but his eyes were bright and keen.

Colonel Dee stood behind his desk and fluttered his hand. 'You going to sit down, Mr Bolder?' he said.

'Sure, I'll sit down.' Mav sat across from the colonel, taking care to keep his back straight.

'Been expecting you,' the colonel said. 'Glad to see you're recovering from your ordeal. Would you care to take a glass of rye?'

'I don't think so,' Mav said. 'I'm here on business.'

Colonel Dee nodded grimly. 'You did a brave thing,' he said. 'I have to admit that.'

Mav held his head on one side. 'Brave or foolish. That's no never mind to me. Now it's pay-back time and I've come to collect my reward' — he paused — 'and ask a few unanswered questions.'

Colonel Dee nodded again. 'About that reward, Mr Bolder — '

Mav tapped on the colonel's desk with his fingers. 'There's no about anything here, Colonel. There's just the matter of three thousand dollars.'

Colonel Dee studied Mav for a moment or two. Then he nodded, pulled open a drawer of his desk and took out an envelope. He slid the envelope across his desk. 'As you see, I have it ready. Three thousand, like you said.'

Mav took the envelope and stowed it in the pocket of his pants. 'I guess you thought I'd be too busy eating desert sand to claim this,' he said. 'Fact is you didn't expect it and you didn't want it.' He was looking directly into the colonel's eyes as he spoke.

Colonel Dee gave an ungracious shrug. 'What makes you say that? Any man's worthy of his pay. We made a deal.'

Mav was grinning. 'Figured I was getting in your hair, didn't you?'

Colonel Dee chuckled. 'Nobody gets in my hair, Mr Bolder. I don't let that happen. What are the few questions you mentioned?'

Mav paused. 'The first is this,' he said. 'I guess you had a hunch those killers would rob the stage. That's why you had that strongbox loaded with rocks.'

Colonel Dee gave him a smug grin. 'Just a hunch, Mr Bolder. Just a hunch. That's how I survive, through guesses and hunches.'

'That particular hunch caused the death of four innocent men and women,' Mav said. 'Not to mention several Comanche braves, but I guess you wouldn't count them anyway.'

'That's consequences, Mr Bolder. I couldn't know any of that would happen. I'm a man of business. A man of business has to look after his business interests.' He nodded briefly and looked up. 'What's the second question?'

Mav stretched his legs under the

desk. 'You call me Jesse Bolder. How come you knew my real name and what have you got against Jesse Bolder so you wanted him dead?'

Colonel Dee put his hand into the drawer again and paused. Could be he's going to pull a gun on me and finish the job! Mav thought. But the colonel took out a faded news sheet and spread it on his desk.

'That's two questions in one, Mr Bolder,' he said. 'And I can answer them both.'

There was a long pause. Then the colonel stirred himself. 'From time to time I read the papers, Mr Bolder, and it tells me here about a fire back in Tennessee, how a woman called Mrs Bolder got burned to death and how a man called Bob Carvill died of a gunshot wound in suspicious circumstances, and how her son, Jesse Bolder, was wanted for the murder of Bob Carvill.' He shook the news sheet. 'It says right here that this man Jesse was thought to have gone West to escape the law. It says he probably has an alias.' He prodded the news sheet with his index finger. 'And there's even a grainy photograph of him here.'

He pushed the paper over to Mav and Mav studied it for a moment. It wasn't exactly a good likeness, but it would do.

'I understand,' Mav said. 'You wanted to turn me in to get me out of your hair?'

Colonel Dee was grinning smugly behind his desk. 'Nobody gets in my hair, Mr Bolder, as I said. If I want something, I go for it. That's business.'

'So there could be another reason,' Mav suggested.

The colonel drummed on the top of his desk for a moment. 'Matter of blood and honour.' He looked Mav directly in the eye. 'You see, Bob Carvill was my cousin. A week before he was killed he wrote me a letter saying he feared for his life. That's how I know.'

'Matter of interest, I didn't kill Bob Carvill,' Mav said. 'I threw him out the window, that's for sure, and I wanted to kill him, but I didn't pull the trigger. Somebody else did that. Somebody with a grudge. And my guess is Carvill deserved it. He probably burned the house down and killed my ma.'

'So that's your story,' the colonel said.

'That's what happened, Colonel.' Mav stood up. 'As for blood and honour, you paid a heavy price for that.'

The colonel watched as Mav turned and walked right out of his office.

★　★　★

Colonel Dee wasn't exactly expecting Letitia, so he was wearing his second best coat when she came. He looked up and saw his secretary showing her in and a thought flashed across his mind: had Letitia come to repent at last? Had she seen the light? Would she agree to be his wife at last?

'Good to see you, Letitia,' he said, giving her a slight imitation of a bow.

'You did a brave but foolhardy thing riding out with that woman Brassy Baby to help Jesse Bolder apprehend those killers.'

'I've come to say goodbye, Colonel,' she said.

The colonel's eyebrows shot up. 'You're not leaving, Letitia?'

'I'm pulling out, Colonel. Leaving on the Butterfield stage tomorrow morning. The cabin's in good order and I'm already packed. So this is goodbye.'

The colonel stood and looked at her in astonishment. What he saw was a new woman, a woman he had scarcely caught a glimpse of before.

'Well, Letitia, I hope you know what you're doing,' he said.

'Life's full of guesses and I think I do,' she said.

★   ★   ★

Next morning the Butterfield stage was loading up. There were more passengers than usual. These included the two

265

actors, Sadie Solomon and Joe Basnett, Brassy Baby, and Gladness herself.

Since the incident with the stage and the shoot-out, Sadie and Joe Basnett had been resting up in the Cimarron Grand. Both had been struck badly by the tragedy and without the two other actors, especially Humphrey, the Abe Lincoln lookalike, they couldn't make up their minds what to do next.

Brassy Baby had pulled out of the the Cimarron Grand. She had moved in with Gladness for a day or two. When she looked in on the hotel to gather some of her things the other girls had given her the cold-shoulder treatment. Who did she think she was? Did she think she was fit to go up in the world and strike poses like that?

As she was hauling her carpetbag through the lobby she encountered Sadie.

'How you doing?' she asked.

'Things are a little bit better,' Sadie told her. 'Joe's been half crazy with grief but he's beginning to pull himself together now that those cruel welts on his back have started to heal.'

'So what's your next move?' Sadie asked.

Sadie gave her a sidelong glance. 'It's time we moved out, I guess. So we're heading for Santa Fe on the stage in the next few days. Sad thing is our company's broken and we can't go on unless we join up with someone else.'

As Brassy Baby nodded with sympathy, a sudden thought flashed across her mind. Though it seemed a crazy notion, she suddenly had a picture of herself acting on a big stage. She saw her name in lights spread right across the top of a huge theatre.

'I've thought about acting,' she said in a quiet, confidential tone. 'Used to think I might be on the stage some day.'

Sadie's eyes came round to focus on her and she seemed to catch a glimpse of Brassy Baby's dream. 'Why don't you come along? Can't promise anything but you might fit in. Pulling the curtain and stuff, placing the chairs and the props.'

Brassy Baby's eyes widened. 'Could I do that?'

'Why not?' Sadie said. 'Some great actors and actresses have started that way. It can happen. Learn as you go along.'

That settled Brassy Baby and that was why she was waiting for the stagecoach that morning.

Gladness and Brassy Baby had talked all night. By morning Gladness had decided to leave her rented house. A good lady who loved dogs took Sheridan and offered her a reasonable price for the furnishings. She might even be prepared to take the lease off her hands. Maybe she had an eye on Colonel Dee. Gladness pitied her for that, but the good woman was a widow and had lived in Cimarron for long enough to know what she was getting herself into. So Gladness took her chance. That was why she was climbing aboard the Butterfield stage.

'My, that's a handsome bunch of womankind,' Stan Baldock sighed as the stage pulled out, headed for Santa Fe.

★　★　★

A little later the same day Josh was astride the mule without a name who was now called 'Singing Mule'.

'You know what, Mr Maverick,' he said. 'I thought one time you and Miss Gladness was set to get hitched. The way she looked at you I knew she'd say yes.'

Mav was riding close and he shook his head. 'You can't expect happy endings all the time,' he said laconically. 'Miss Gladness is in no state to say yes to any man. Could be she will one day. Who can tell?'

He and Josh had watched as the Butterfield stage pulled out for Santa Fe. The night before, Mav and Gladness had sat out under the ramada looking up at the stars with their drinks.

'You think you're doing the right thing?' he asked her.

'I'm doing the only thing,' she said. 'When I look up at those stars I see my little children and my late husband beckoning to me and I know I have to go on.'

Mav figured Gladness might never marry again and he figured he wasn't the marrying kind, anyway.

That was what he was thinking about as Gladness turned at the door of the stage and waved her hand in goodbye, and that was what he was thinking about now as he and Josh rode back along the trail.

'You know what, man?' Josh said to Mav. 'I dun got dollars in my pocket thanks to you and Miss Letitia and a mule under my body, also thanks to you. And I'm on my way home. Tell them I'm coming. I'm on my way!' He raised his eyes to the clouds and shouted: 'Tell them I'm coming. Alleluia!' He started to sing in a deep melodious tone. Singing Mule opened his mouth and gave a loud not-very-melodious bray, possibly in agreement.

At the parting of the trail, Mav and Josh paused for a moment. This was where they must say *adios*.

'Why, thank you for Singing Mule, Mr Mav,' Josh sang out, 'and thanks for the dollars. They'll set me up real good when I get back there.' He turned his dark, laughing eyes on Mav. 'Why don't you come along too, Mr Mav? We'll give you a real good time.'

Mav gave him a wide grin. 'Thanks for the offer, Mr Josh. That would be an honour, but I have other plans.'

'None of my business, but what other plans would they be, Mr Mav?'

Mav raised one eyebrow. 'I'll send you a letter when I get there,' he said.

'You do that, Mr Mav.' Josh laughed. They both knew that Josh couldn't read and Mav didn't have his address anyway.

Josh sat in the saddle and watched as Mav rode slowly towards the West.

'That Mav was a real good man,' he

said aloud, 'a real good man, you know that, Singing Mule?'

Then he turned towards the East and started to sing his alleluias again.

THE END

We do hope that you have enjoyed reading this large print book.

Did you know that all of our titles are available for purchase?

We publish a wide range of high quality large print books including:
Romances, Mysteries, Classics
General Fiction
Non Fiction and Westerns

Special interest titles available in large print are:
The Little Oxford Dictionary
Music Book, Song Book
Hymn Book, Service Book

Also available from us courtesy of Oxford University Press:
Young Readers' Dictionary
(large print edition)
Young Readers' Thesaurus
(large print edition)

For further information or a free brochure, please contact us at:
Ulverscroft Large Print Books Ltd.,
The Green, Bradgate Road, Anstey,
Leicester, LE7 7FU, England.
Tel: (00 44) **0116 236 4325**
Fax: (00 44) **0116 234 0205**

Other titles in the
Linford Western Library:

HIDEOUT AT MENDER'S CROSSING

John Glasby

The ghost town of Mender's Crossing is the ideal base for a gang of outlaws operating without interference. When a group of soldiers is killed defending a gold-train, the army calls upon special operator Steve Landers to investigate. However, Landers is also up against land baron Hal Clegg: his hired mercenaries are driving independent ranchers from their land. He will need nerves of steel to succeed when he is so heavily outnumbered. Can he cheat the odds and win?